MYSTERIES AND STRANGE EVENTS

by

Drew Jones

CONTENTS

INTRODUCTION FROM THE AUTHOR

Welcome to Volume Two of Mysteries and Strange Events. I am Drew Jones and I have really had fun putting this new four story collection together – so I hope you will enjoy them too.

This particular set was produced during the lockdown and so perhaps it will help you to pass an hour or so during your solitude.

.

THE DISAPPEARANCES AT BLADE ROCK LIGHTHOUSE

Britain's remote rock lighthouses-built generations ago and designed to withstand the brutal unforgiving sea. Although now all are devoid of human keepers, they remain working to this day protecting shipping with their welcoming guiding light and seeing them safely on their way.

Five men are dropped at one such lighthouse to carry out important work - as a storm suddenly rolls in, they discover a much greater danger awaits them inside.

March 22 1995

The sea resembled a sheet of dark blue glass on that fateful day as a solitary helicopter headed further out over its calm vastness. The sky was pale blue, cloudless and radiating warmth.

The coastline and breaking waves were soon left far behind as the noisy machine churned the peaceful air and continued on. After a few minutes, it deviated from its original course, started to circle, and then gradually lost height. Its destination was now clear, a collection of gaunt black jagged rocks lay directly below - they numbered five in total. A much larger rock then came into view, it had been made flat in the middle with deeply carved out steps leading down into the sea. The remains of a landing stage were at one end, while perched on its southern edge was a lonely pale coloured lighthouse.

The bright red helicopter hovered over the lighthouse then started to descend and gently touched down on the weathered helipad. Five men in bright orange immersion suits disembarked and started unloading equipment, one bent down and opened a heavy yellow hatch leading to the lamp gallery. Equipment and other items were passed back and fore then after a few more minutes the helipad was vacated and the helicopter noisily departed and eventually peace returned.

The five men are engineers, dropped at this lonely tower to convert it to automation, they now represent the entire population of Blade Rock lighthouse.

"Go below Andrew and get things sorted, oh and a cup of tea would be good!"

"No problem Ian leave it to me, oh and hey, what did your last slave die of?"

The other three men sniggered as Andrew carefully clambered down the steps and disappeared into the cramped interior of the lighthouse carrying his kit bag. The eldest of the five was called Sam, he stood on the helipad and surveyed it carefully then called over to one of his colleagues.

"Donald, can you and Tony go and check that the rest of the equipment that was dropped yesterday, has been stowed properly, this is going to be a long lonely job."

Blade Rock lighthouse was situated a little over 5 miles off the Cornish coast - the first lighthouse was partly destroyed in a monumental storm sometime around 1858 leaving no survivors, or in fact much of the structure. It wasn't until 1875 that the current granite tower was finally completed and it had stood the test of time and the unrelenting pounding seas ever since. It was 47 meters high; construction was based closely on John Smeaton's tested idea of granite dovetails giving enormous strength to the structure. The walls started off as thick as eight feet at the bottom gradually diminishing as the tower rose. The layout of Blade Rock lighthouse was thus:

The 1st floor consisted of a tank for fresh drinking water located in the base.

The 2nd floor was the narrow entrance room with a

ladder leading down into the tank below. The height from the entrance door to the granite base below was well over 20 feet. The interior stairs leading to each level at Blade Rock were very steep, made from black painted metal with a thick rope fastened to the wall to act as a handrail.

The 3rd floor housed several large tanks containing diesel fuel with a hand pump to transfer fuel upstairs.

The 4th floor housed the engine room, two diesel engines and generators situated side by side, one would be running with the other in a state of readiness. The chatter from the running engine could be heard throughout the lighthouse.

The 5th floor contained more fuel tanks, a tiny shower and flushing toilet, there were also many storage racks attached to the walls.

The 6th floor was a small kitchen area arranged in a semi-circle as you would expect. Cupboards were almost all the way around the room at head height and there was also a small table and chairs for the now redundant keepers to sit at during meal times.

7th floor housed the sleeping quarters. There were enough beds for five men in total, these were known as "banana bunks" due to them being curved to match the contours of the walls. Each bunk had its own emergency life support apparatus (ELSA) hung above it in a bright orange bag.

The 8th floor was almost unique to this lighthouse it contained a sitting room. There were three armchairs and a table neatly arranged, a tv, a video recorder and a well-stocked bookshelf. Not many UK lighthouses had this extra room. Here was also located the radio sets to call the helicopter and another set for all other contact.

The 9th floor was the service room or another engine room but much more cramped. It housed two more diesel generators and there were also eight or nine compressed air tanks suspended from the ceiling. These were used to run the fog horns, and this room also contained the station batteries.

The final floor was, of course, the lamp or lens room, and, depending on the size of the lens, this could stretch over two levels, as was the case with Blade Rocks. There were ladders leading to a catwalk giving access to the lamp itself and further on up to the helipad. There were also two electric motors in this room.

The Blade Rock lighthouse had a range of 25 nautical miles which gave two white flashes every 15 seconds. The three protruding fog horns resembled oversized trumpets and would give two blasts every 60 seconds when needed. As with most offshore rock lighthouses, Blade Rock had had a helipad fitted, in around 1978. This made replenishing supplies and crew change delays due to the notoriously bad weather and surprise squalls, a thing of the past. The conversion to automation had been delayed by nearly two years due to a fire at another lighthouse taking priority. The operators of Blade Rock had made suitable arrangements for shipping while the light was briefly out of commission.

The wind speed was beginning to increase as the last of the equipment was brought down and crammed in the restricted confines of the ancient lighthouse or secured on the narrow catwalk outside.

"Tea up boys," called Andrew from the confines of the cosy kitchen. Tony appeared first and quickly made himself at home in the best chair - "Nice one mate, the others will be right down."

Donald then appeared and sat at the small table. "It's blowing up outside, yet 30 minutes ago it looked almost like summer - oh, is this my tea - thanks. Ian says can you take his and Sam's up to the living room?"

Andrew raised his eyes to heaven and made his way up two flights of stairs to deliver the steaming tea.

"Your tea sirs, I didn't spill a drop" he quipped as he entered the snug little living room and set the chunky mugs down on the oak table.

"Thanks Andrew we'll be down in a minute, how're things looking below? Engines ok?"

"Yeah Sam all ship-shape and polished, it must have been a sad day for the keepers to leave after all this time."

The comment drew little response from Sam and Ian and with that Andrew descended back down to the kitchen to re-join Tony and Donald.

"They will be down in a minute or so, gees those stairs are steep, we better start getting some of these windows closed before the storm hits."

Andrew interrupted Tony and Donald who were halfway through a conversation about expensive cars, Tony was a confirmed "petrol head" and was discussing his next purchase. Donald was feigning an interest but much preferred his private boat moored in Norfolk. Heavy clambering on the metal steps announced the arrival of Sam and Ian, they squeezed into the kitchen and put their empty mugs in the sink. Sam, who was in charge of the work to be undertaken was about to issue instructions when a perturbed Donald interrupted him.

"Shhh, what's that? I can hear footsteps from below," he said.

The other four men all turned to face the curved wooden glass panelled door and listened intently, the hum of the bottom diesel engine was the prominent sound. Andrew then spoke.

"God your right, something is moving about down there. What do you make of it Sam?"

As the five men listened, sure enough, heavy thuds and footsteps could be heard, after about 10 seconds these sounds ceased and were replaced by the sound of the strengthening gusts of howling wind.

Sam quickly responded with a volley of questions and instructions.

"You are sure all of the keepers left just before we got here Andrew? Did you see anything odd when you first went down there? Are the main doors open?"

But by this time Andrew had gone to the top of the stairs and was already looking down to the next level with intrigue.

"The helicopter pilot told me he had picked them all up an hour before we arrived in the other helicopter to save time as ours was full up with equipment. As for anything strange, no not at all, one engine running nicely and yes, the main doors were open, it didn't strike me as odd, they were probably letting some air through the place and getting rid of condensation," he answered.

Sam nodded his agreement and then waved his hand almost in disgust at the amount of time he had wasted on such a trivial matter.

"Forget it you blokes, we have enough to worry about - Tony you and Andrew go below and turn off that engine. Ian go upstairs and switch on one of the little generators, that will do us for now. Oh, and you two also close those main entrance doors or we'll have five feet of water down there by the sound of it outside."

The group then dispersed and went about their various tasks, although the mysterious sounds from below were hard to shake off. Tony and Andrew descended the near vertical steps until they reached the toilet and shower room, another descent brought them to the always closed engine room door. Andrew turned the handle and they both walked in.

"Nothing, just as I told Sam," Andrew said while

switching off the droning engine.

"Yeah, God knows what that was all about but let's hope it was just Blade Rock welcoming us!" Tony quipped. The two men then climbed down past the oil tank room and carried on until they arrived at the main doors. Before closing them and replacing the metal supports, they climbed down some twenty feet using the rusty metal "dog steps" until they reach the gargantuan granite base. From this, another set of steps (offset from the ones they had just used) descended again to give access to the black barnacle-encrusted rock itself, but the sea was too rough to entertain using these. The massive base was stained a dirty grey in most places courtesy of the relentless sea. The two men completed a full circuit of the base with the aid of a hefty guide rope fixed to the wall of the tower.

"No mermaids or anyone else," chirped Tony. By now the sea was hitting the base hard and white foam spray was reaching as high as the entrance door. Andrew glanced up at the massive tower, the granite blocks were flaking in places, a rusty line almost akin to an unsightly scar ran down the full length of the tower. This was caused by eroded bolts that held the copper lightning conductor in its channel. Shouting to be heard over the fierce wind he turned to Tony.

"Come on let's get back up, it's getting worse by the minute!"

Once back inside the entrance room the two closed and bolted the doors and then put each of the supports in place. When they reached the first oil tank room Andrew stopped to take a reading of the fuel levels and told Tony to go on up and report to Sam that all was ok and secure below. The other three men were already starting to strip out redundant equipment in the top engine room when Tony gave his report, this was acknowledged and then he was asked to take the five men's personal luggage to the bedroom.

Outside the sky was darkening, the peaceful clear blue that heralded their arrival on this collection of feared desolate rocks had been relegated to a mere memory. The men carried on with their assigned tasks as the storm front continued building...

"So, where the hell is Tony then?" Sam asked the others in the kitchen.

"It's obvious" replied Donald, "his idea of stowing the luggage is to fall asleep in his bunk!" Ian bounded up the stairs two at a time to the bedroom level and angrily pushed open the door, the top bunk on the left-hand side was the only one to have its curtain drawn across it.

"Tony get up, what the hell are you playing at? We need help up there!" concurrently with saying this he hurled back the curtains... the bunk was perfectly empty and still freshly made.

"What the..." he mumbled. He glanced around the tiny room and then darted back down the stairs.

"He's not there, just his suitcase and car magazines."

The four men looked at each other dumbfounded. Sam asked Donald and Andrew to go down to the lower levels and see what he was doing. He reasoned he wasn't any further up than the bedroom as he had not long come from there himself. By now it was late afternoon and darkness had enveloped the isolated lighthouse. The wind was still picking up speed outside and the sound of the angry sea colliding against the black razor-sharp rocks and granite base went on unrelentingly.

"He's not down there Sam, the entrance is still secure," Donald quietly reported. He looked nervous and pale and there was a distinct tremor in his voice. Sam asked if he was sure they had checked everywhere including the shower cubicle - Donald nodded then slumped back against one of the kitchen cupboards.

"This is ridiculous, it's a lighthouse, not a stately home he can't have gone far, I last saw him when he and I locked the door and went to the engine room, how long has elapsed since then?" Andrew asked.

"40 or 45 minutes no more, our luggage has all been stowed in the bedroom so he must have done that much," came the reply from Ian.

Just then the men's deliberations were broken by a dragging sound from one of the levels below, it was impossible to distinguish which, due to the howling wind and turmoil outside. As before they once again huddled in the kitchen listening. For a second there seemed to be what sounded like a muffled voice then the definite sound of heavy footfall on the metal steps, after this all sounds stopped from below…

"Tony will you stop f****** about and get up here!" Ian bellowed down the steps.

"I told you no one was down there" came an edgy comment from Donald as he scanned the eyes of the others. The four of them then made the trip back down to the entrance door, it was still securely fastened obviously ruling out any possibility of Tony having left the tower that way.

"Well then, he evidently got past us in the top engine room and is in the lamp room," was Sam's conclusive reply to the others. The lamp room when visited also drew a blank, they were greeted with only an icy chill and sheets of rain being driven against the glass windows with a deafening pinging sound.

"Don't be stupid you can't go any further, it's too dangerous to go up top in this storm you're be blown clean off the pad in the blink of an eye," Andrew shouted to Donald who was already halfway up the ladder leading to the hatch that gave access to the helipad. Sam then intervened,

"He's right, knock it off Donald before you get yourself killed - if Tony were up there… well, let's just say he can't be up there in this."

Donald slowly climbed down the ladder and re-joined the others, after a few seconds he spoke.

"He's dead then you mean?"

Sam didn't answer but asked everyone to wait in the

kitchen while he went to the living room to radio base for instructions on the situation.

Donald, Andrew and Ian sat in silence at the little kitchen table. Each man seemed to be working out a logical reason as to why Tony would want to go up onto the helipad in the middle of a storm. Had he left something up there, gone to retrieve it, and been swept to his doom by a gust of wind? And what of those eerie sounds that had emanated from below? No one could deny they actually had been heard. Ian was just about to speak when Sam came down from the living room shaking his head.

"The radio isn't working at all… I've tried every channel".

This latest revelation served only to compound the sad depressing atmosphere that pervaded the lighthouse. Ian banged his fist on the table and then got up so fast it sent the skinny dining chair toppling over backwards. He paced to the door then looked at Sam,

"How about using the set for the helicopter, don't tell me that's not f****** working either? My cell phone will be useless out here so that does it!" Before responding, Sam asked Andrew to make them all a cup of coffee then picked up the chair and sat down.

"First thing I tried after having no luck with the other set," he solemnly announced and then rubbed his forehead with his right hand in a fatigued manner. Andrew brought the mugs of piping hot coffee over to the table and another awkward unnerving silence blanketed the kitchen. Every now and then a wind-accelerated wave would be driven against the base and side of the tower causing it to shudder and vibrate. To anyone not used to working on an offshore lighthouse, this would have caused great concern but the four men had become accustomed to it. Sam took a few sips of his drink which seem to rouse him from his gloom.

"The supply helicopter will be calling again tomorrow at 1pm anyway so the radio situation has not affected the current state of affairs in any way, there is nothing we can do until they get here, especially in this storm. Tony should have known better than to go out like that, I'm sorry it happened but it's done with."

This rather less than charitable summing up of the situation seemed oddly to rally the other three for the time being, although Donald still seemed unnerved and panicky. He cleared his throat and then in a rasping voice spoke.

"They say this lighthouse is haunted, a curse hangs over the place - ever since the older tower was destroyed." But before he could say any more Ian rudely interrupted him.

"Shut it Donald, we don't need ghost stories on top of what was obviously a careless accident!" and with that he scowled at the withdrawn man. Andrew broke the rising tension by getting up and going over to the food cupboards.

"I'll open a few tins of something and get dinner on, sounds silly but it might make us feel better," he said.

Outside the howling wind screamed vengeance on the lighthouse, continuing its onslaught on the walls and windows of the structure. The sea around the base of the forsaken tower seemed to be boiling white as it thundered and crashed around the rocks below. Every so often a massive wave would dwarf the base and slam into the structure reaching as high as the 4th or 5th floor then receding back into the depths. The violent gusts of wind would catch the top of the foamy water and violently spit it at the granite walls as if furious at the structures ability to withstand its attack.

Straight after dinner, Donald left the others to go to his bunk, he seemed to drag his feet and took forever ascending the stairs to the bedroom on the next level.

"We will have to watch him you two," Ian whispered to the others. "There will be a big fuss over Tony snuffing it, if they interview him and he starts talking rubbish about curses and ghostly footsteps they are bound to think we had all been drinking or playing the fool!"

"Your right Ian, I'll look in on him later it's only just gone 7 now" Sam replied. Andrew also agreed but pointed out that the footsteps and noises had actually occurred and they all heard them on both occasions. They defied all logical explanation…

The chunky polished brass clock showed quarter past nine in the 6th floor kitchen, the air was heavy and condensation ran down the sealed windows. With the exception of Donald, the other three had stayed in the kitchen to write out clear statements on the events leading up to Tony's disappearance. Sam had told the other two to leave out any mention of the inexplicable sounds they had all heard. Outside wasn't quite as bad but it still showed no signs of easing significantly. Sam collected the statements and put them in an envelope which he then left on top of the microwave oven until Donald's could be added to it. Andrew put the kettle on to boil and then left the other two to head down to the toilet. When he returned the other two were engaged in a half-hearted conversation about Ian's latest venture of buying properties to rent out. They stopped as soon as Andrew entered the room and Sam announced he would go and wake Donald and bring him down for a cup of tea so he could write out his statement.

"He's really got the wind up that he will be blamed for Tony going bye-bye," Ian scoffed.

"You act like you don't care Ian?" The dour conversation was abruptly cut short by Sam's voice shouting in an alarming tone.

"Christ, Ian bring the first aid kit up here, Donald isn't breathing, both of you get up here!" Donald was to be found fully clothed on one of the lower bunks, his face was an off-white, while his lips had a blue tinge about them. It was evident he had been dead for some time…

"Forget trying to render any first aid Sam, the poor sod's been dead for a good hour or more, I thought he looked sickly before he left the kitchen, must have been the shock of Tony," Ian said, then backed away from the corpse.

"What's he doing in that lower bunk? It's mine," Sam asked. Andrew covered the body with a fresh linen bed sheet then replied to Sam's question.

"He must have been so poorly he simply couldn't use the ladder to get up to his bunk, it was almost as if he died within minutes of entering the room." Andrew then barged out of the room and shouted he was going up to look at the radios sets again. The other two followed and turned out the light in the bedroom leaving Donald to his eternal sleep.

"It's beyond a coincidence all this! What's the matter with the damn things, they both look in perfect condition?" Andrew had removed the back of both sets and the other two agreed nothing seemed missing, burnt out or damaged. Sam told him to leave them for the time being and sit down while they thought about what to do. Ian paced about the living room for a few seconds before he sat down and started tapping the arms of the chair in an agitated manner. In the short time since they had arrived at this desolate outpost, one man was missing presumed dead while a second was confirmed deceased.

Sam lit a cigarette and recapped their position; he was 90 per cent sure Tony had been blown from the helipad while trying to retrieve an item of forgotten luggage or for other reasons unknown. Donald must have died of natural causes, a post mortem would verify that and exonerate them of any suspicion regarding his passing. He surmised he must have had a weak heart or other medical complications; he was in his mid-50's so not unheard of. He then lit another cigarette and stared at the flame from his gold engraved lighter, he was about to carry on with his theories when he suddenly turned to the door.

"It's those bloody footsteps down below again!" he

shouted.

The uneasiness built to a fever pitch as the remaining men listened to the detested footsteps coming from way down below. Ian grabbed a fire axe and headed to the stairs,

"I've had enough of this crap!" Andrew followed him, by this time the sounds had again stopped, all that could be heard was the raging storm from the blackness outside and the rhythmic hum of the diesel generator upstairs. The three men were cut off from the world protected only from certain death by granite stones hewn and assembled well over a century ago but still protecting the occupants of Blade Rock lighthouse, or maybe it would seem, trapping them inside…?

"It's still not easing up outside, not that it will do us any good if it were, God - listen to that wind"

"Your right Sam," replied Andrew, "even if it were a summer day outside it wouldn't change things much." Ian was in a black mood - he wanted to go back down and finally confront whatever was making those mysterious sounds, but they decided to remain in the living room. Occasionally Sam examined the radio while Andrew tried to distract himself from the situation by thumbing through some of the yellowed pages of various books. Eventually, Ian's patience ran out,

"It's gone 11 now, are we going to just sit up all night in here?"

Andrew neatly rested his book down and in a

condescending tone replied,

"No one's stopping you going to bed, I'm sure Donald wouldn't object." Sam got up and rebuked Andrew for such a disrespectful comment.

"I'm sorry Ian, it was a bit low, it's just this whole situation is unbelievable - like a nightmare. Thank God the helicopter is coming tomorrow."

Ian waved a hand as if to say "just forget it" and then Sam suggested they made their way down to the kitchen for a hot drink. The other two agreed and they climbed down past the dark bedroom and then to the kitchen. Before going in, Sam said he was going downstairs to the toilet and to make him a coffee.

Andrew looked perturbed at this suggestion and said, "What about the noises?"

"They are what they are and have no bearing on what's happened, anyway you've been downstairs several times and it's been ok." Andrew conceded the point and told him coffee and biscuits on the table in five minutes. Sam managed a half smile and made his way down to the next level.

The door to the toilet had not even opened half way when a piercing shot rang out echoing through the stone interior. Blood splattered the white paint making it resemble a Jackson Pollock painting. Sam staggered backwards until hitting the wall, he made a gurgling sound, his arms flailed in a deranged motion and then he collapsed at the foot of the metal stairs dead.

"Christ - a shot! Sam! Sam are you there?" Ian was at the stairs looking down in undisguised horror. Andrew picked up a large kitchen knife and joined him.

"He's there! God almighty half his face is missing! Let's get down there."

Andrew looked down at the crumpled body, dark red blood smoked the floor, pellets had ricocheted off the impregnable granite, the acrid smell of gun powder hung in the damp air.

"Don't be a bloody fool Ian! Some lunatic is down there with a shotgun - they will pop us off like clay pigeons if we go down. Can't you see - they were just waiting to ambush the next person to go into that room! Sam just happened to be that person, let's get up to the living room and barricade the door until the helicopter arrives tomorrow." Andrew flung a few items in a small box while Ian waited by the stairs holding a fire axe at the ready, then without speaking a word to each other they scrambled up the stairs past the bedroom and dived into the living room. Once there, they put a chair under the door handle and moved a bookcase in front of it.

"Get it against the wall Andrew, that was a sawn-off shotgun did you see the damage and spread? Someone really wanted to make sure." Andrew didn't reply, instead he checked his watch 11.44, it was still an unbelievably long time until the helicopter would arrive, and he made Ian aware of this obvious fact.

"Forget the time, there could be anyone down there, at

least there is only one door for them to try and get in, just be ready."

The time seemed to drag, with every minute feeling like 20, by 3am the men were exhausted but they knew how dangerous it could be to fall asleep. As long as they stayed awake, they had a chance of repelling the unseen assassin. The storm which had been continuing all this time had been forgotten about in light of the clear and present danger that they now faced inside the tower. It was ironic, to step outside would mean certain death from a crashing wave and being swept away into the icy blackness, but to remain inside also spelt destruction.

Andrew crawled on all fours over to the box he managed to get from the kitchen. The glass panels of the door had been totally covered by the bookcase, should the murderer be waiting on the other side for an easy target - they would be out of luck.

"What are you doing? "Ian whispered while glancing at the barricade to check all was well.

"Getting us some cans of drink, it's well past three I'm worried we will nod off and wake up dead, if you see what I mean?"

"Good idea, I don't want to make it easy for this b*****d". Andrew opened the cans of fizzy orange, he asked Ian to check the door before he reached out and passed him a can.

"Here, this should do the trick mate," he said.

Not a sound stirred from the other side of the door, as with all the other times it was just storm and the generators endless chattering to be heard.

"What are they waiting for Ian? They have a gun why not just start blasting away, it's not like they will disturb the neighbours."

"I was thinking the same thing, I don't know about Donald but it looks like they did for Tony too, God the mess that made of Sam!"

"What do you think our chances are Ian? It doesn't look good does it? It feels like the whole thing has been planned. I bet we have more chance of winning the lottery than getting off Blade Rock alive."

"What do you mean by that?" Ian turned and looked at Andrew and gave him a nervous inquisitive smile. The hours without sleep were obviously gnawing at Ian he felt so drained.

"I was just saying how our situation seems so hopeless that we'd have more chance of our syndicate winning that new-fangled lottery," Andrew explained.

Ian once again took his drooping eyes off the stockade and looked over at Andrew and whispered, "Don't go to pieces mate, we still have a…" he nodded slightly and took a long blink. "We still have a chance," he finally managed to say.

Andrew glanced down at his watch, it was now 4 am. Ian had stopped clutching the fire axe some time ago and was visibly struggling to stay awake.

"Ian are you ok? I hope I didn't ramble on too much a little while ago? It's not like I'd ever win the lottery, I guess that always happens to other people, don't you think?"

Ian was slowly rocking, his eyes now closed and his face expressionless.

"Ian? Have you fallen asleep? You said you weren't going to make it easy for the killer, Ian?"

The hostile environment outside continued on, cascades of rain peppered the sealed windows, the sea shook the lighthouse as it had done for decade after decade, while inside the confining cold stone walls only one man was now conscious...

Ian struggled to open his eyes he could feel the cold wind on his back, his head was pounding, he felt like throwing up any second. Panic gripped him when he realised he could not move his arms or legs, they felt numb. Slowly his eyelids lifted and a huge grey expanse came in and out of focus. Panic turned to undiluted terror when the sheer scale of his situation dawned upon him. He had woken up tied to one of the kitchen chairs and was out on the helipad. It was light outside, and the grey expanse his eyes had struggled to comprehend, was the churning featureless sea. His ankles had been trussed up tightly to each chair leg with heavy-duty tape, while his arms had been crossed over and placed behind the back of the chair and securely bound at the wrist with a thick cable-tie. He was as helpless as a new-born baby, and he rocked at regular intervals as a gust of wind caught him.

After a few minutes, he could hear the hatch open behind him, he daren't risk trying to turn around in case the chair went from under him and he ended up face first on the pad.

"Who's there? Is someone there? Andrew - is that you? Get me out of here!"

The unidentified personage approached, it was only a matter of five or six steps until they were directly behind the restrained pathetic looking man...

"Hello Ian, it's me" came at last.

"Christ Andrew, it is you! What happened? Look, get me out of here before whoever did this comes back up, did you see them? Have you already stopped them? I remember feeling sleepy in the living room then I woke up here." Andrew walked round to face Ian, he had something under his arm, before he spoke, he set it down.

"Get you out of here? It's taken me long enough to drag you up here." Then came silence and both men stared at each other.

"Would you surprise me and just for once do ME a favour Ian please? I know you're not used to doing things for other people but just oblige me this once." Ian didn't reply his confused hurting head was trying to work out what was happening.

"Sorry Ian, I'm being selfish, let me move you closer to the edge, you will get a better view, always a sea view on a lighthouse." Andrew grabbed the back of the chair and dragged it over to near the edge of the helipad. A small portion of the net which supposedly stops objects being blown off the pad had been cut away.

"No don't - stop please!" Ian called out and struggled to break out of the chair. Andrew then pulled an envelope sized piece of white paper from his pocket and unfolded it.

"Now the favour, please read these numbers out." To make sure he complied he nodded the base of the chair with his foot causing it to rock, which in turn caused Ian to call out in terror.

"Ok, ok, I'll do it."

The paper had six numbers written on it in black marker pen. Ian paused for two or three seconds then recited the numbers.

"**5, 9, 11, 23, 36, 42**" Ian's voice trembled. As soon as he had finished, Andrew let the paper go from his thumb and forefinger causing it to immediately travel on the wind out to sea.

"Oh my God you know, I can explain Andrew, just give me a minute!" Andrew pushed the base of the chair with his foot again, Ian shrieked and immediately stopped talking.

"I've looked forward to telling the last survivor how I made my discovery and how I went about ridding the world of back-stabbing trash, now shut up until I tell you to speak!" Ian nodded; his face was as pale as Donald's had been in death.

"I first realised you and your buddies had conned me about three months ago. I was up in Wales on another automation job, one of the old keepers there was an avid gambler he had formulas for everything. One lunchtime I came across his permutations for the lottery so naturally, I asked him to explain his theories and had he had any luck. The numbers I had been staring at had been the winning numbers since the lottery had started, from these results he then studied the frequency etc and looked for patterns. It was the line of recent numbers two down from the top that caught my eye, **36** and **42** that's been yours and mine for ages Ian."

Ian went to call out but this was instantly quashed by Andrew raising his foot. He then went on -

"I noted the numbers out of interest, it didn't take my investigations long to discover that a syndicate wishing to remain anonymous had one £3.8 million a few weeks earlier. I checked the numbers a week later with our beloved lottery treasurer Sam to make sure he hadn't changed them since we started. When he said he hadn't the bottom fell out of my world. I had been such a bloody fool! Donald buying a 30-foot yacht, Tony and his endless fast cars and you with your property portfolio! You were still all talking about the things you had bought right up until yesterday! But at least you had the good grace to always stop when I came into the room!" Andrew was consumed with anger and kicked the base of the chair hard causing it to violently nod and move backwards, had a gust of wind caught it at that precise moment it may well have gone over the edge.

"No stop! Please Andrew let me explain, please I'm begging you." Andrew roared with laughter at the other man's whimpers.

"Yes, please do explain how you conned me out of my share, I'd love to hear it"

"You hadn't paid your money that week, so when the numbers came up, we all agreed you had to be in it to win it. We had all paid but you didn't bother, you must remember that."

"Is that it? That's what you're using in defence of me not kicking you off this edge? I knew you were a shallow dickhead Ian but this is good even for you! If YOU remember that week, I had been called away urgently to visit my stepmother in Scotland she was dying of cancer, oddly enough paying Sam one pound before I left didn't cross my mind!"

Ian had tears streaming down his face, he was desperately trying to anchor his feet to the surface of the helipad, the chair was just a handful of inches from the edge.

"Save the tears it means nothing to me, oh and by the way when I returned from visiting my stepmother, I paid Sam two pounds, one for the week I missed and one for the next draw, the asshole actually took my money and thanked me! My stepmother died nearly seven weeks ago in some crappy understaffed run-down end of life establishment. Had I been a rich man I could have afforded for a 24-hour private nurse to stay in her own home, but of course I'm not a rich man, am I Ian!"

Huge banks of white clouds with dark grey edges were moving fast overhead, spits of rain started for a few seconds and then stopped just as abruptly, the cream coloured water swirled around the jagged rocks and base of the lighthouse.

"Now Ian, the executions… they were planned in great detail and I must say I'm delighted with how it all went. I always hoped you or Sam would be the last one alive, I didn't care who I killed first out of the other two." Andrew paced the helipad then bent down and picked up the grey box-shaped object and pressed a button with his thumb.

"Christ, the noises they were all on tape!" Ian called out in a chilling voice.

"In order for me to keep you four scumbags guessing until I took your lives, I needed to have an edge, something that would muddy the waters and clear me of any wrongdoing. I recorded the footfalls and echoes in a disused factory near where I live. The one biggest fear I had was someone hearing the noises and running down to investigate and finding the tape machine and speaker. So with that in mind, I produced three looped tapes with huge gaps in-between, a few seconds worth of sounds, or in some cases, a huge timed gap first then the sounds, then nothing."

Andrew chuckled as the familiar footsteps once again played over, then without warning, he hurled the tape player over the side. The heavy footsteps were still in progress when the machine hit the turbulent water and disappeared.

The full impact of just how much effort Andrew had put into the scheme of things had only just begun to dawn on Ian. He sat strapped to the chair with an equal mixture of disbelief and shock realisation. Andrew walked up close to Ian and rested his heavy work boot on the edge of the chair,

"You very obligingly ordered me downstairs to make tea the moment we landed; this was perfect for my plan. I took my kit bag and headed straight to the lower oil tanks, I hid a shotgun and some metal poles behind one tank and set up the tape recorder behind the other, taking care to discreetly hide the extra speaker I would need for the sounds to be heard over the diesel engine. I selected a tape that would start off with silence for 20 minutes then there would be 12 seconds of noises. Next, I quickly made my way up to the radio sets and unscrewed the backs of both and replaced one circuit board in each with identical faulty ones, any close scrutiny would not spot this. Andrew gleefully recounted to a broken Ian how they had all stood in the kitchen the first time as the phantom of Blade Rock was heard downstairs…

"It wasn't hard disposing of Tony; we made a check outside and around the base, which of course revealed nothing. I sent him up to report his findings to our genial leader for two reasons: one, I wanted to switch tapes over and two, I wanted you and Sam to be the last to have seen him, I think that's what's called misdirecting people. Hapless Tony hadn't long finished stowing gear in the bedroom when I called him back down to the oil tank room. I told him to try the hand pump as there was a problem sending fuel up, as he bent down to look at it, I cracked his skull with an enormous spanner out of the engine room tool chest."

Andrew paused to light a cigarette he cupped his hands and turned his back to the wind to accomplish this.

"Please, I don't want to hear any more" Ian snivelled.

"Where was I? oh yes disposal, I dropped Tony out onto the base and pushed him over the south side, you've no idea the mess he made on the granite, I didn't bother to clean it up, the sea would do that for me at no extra cost. I expect he will drift ashore somewhere; most turds do."

Ian struggled fruitlessly in the chair - Andrew watched in silence then after a while pointed down to the chair legs to remind him his puny efforts were only serving to move him closer to his doom.

"That wet lettuce Donald played right into my hands by getting all sweaty over the sounds from below. I managed to press the play button on my hidden machine while he and I were searching below. I sent him to check the shower cubicle and just got it done in time, I had 10 minutes before eight seconds worth of noises would start up. It worked out brilliantly as we were all once again in the kitchen when the ghosts made their second cacophony. By the time we all made our way down, there was just white noise on the tape which was drowned out by the storm outside. Once Sam had wrongly diagnosed that Tony had died from being blown off the helipad, I very thoughtfully made us all a meal, tinned beef stew and potatoes. Donald's food was of course laced with enough crushed sleeping pills to kill three adults. I was pleasantly surprised when he managed to make it upstairs to the bedroom - I had expected him to collapse at the table and have to go through a lengthy tiresome performance of trying to save his life."

Another storm front was approaching from the west, a dark ribbon of cloud was on the horizon the bitter wind was once again picking up speed. Gulls squealed overhead and made towards the sanctuary of the coastal cliffs. Ian's head hung down; he couldn't take anymore but was forced to endure more torment.

"Sam, our trusted supervisor, what a hypocrite, was it his idea or yours to cut me out? Anyway, I'm sure even your walnut sized brain has worked out by now I had jerry-rigged a shotgun to go off in his face as he opened the door. This would not only give him the death he deserved but also look as if the owner of the unexplained footsteps had turned nasty. After he had us write out statements, I said I was going to the toilet. I quickly assembled a device that I had constructed to hold the shotgun in place, and to get the balance right I had already cut four inches off the barrel. Once erected it resembled a sturdy camera tripod, I was able to tape it onto the lid of the toilet seat and angle the barrel to roughly face height. I then all but closed the door just leaving enough space for me to squeeze through. Next,

I tied a string around the door handle the other was of course tied to the trigger of the gun. I had adjusted the pull of the shotgun to the point where it had the world's worst hair trigger - if even a mouse farted in that room it could go off. I loaded one barrel with a mild cartridge to minimise damage to the walls etc and then prayed I did not disturb the door as I ducked down and left the room. The slightest change in the position of the door in any direction would cause enough movement on the trigger to discharge the weapon. Sounds complicated but I had rehearsed it at home at least 10 times. Finally, for the last time I selected one final tape to play, the sounds would start after 15 minutes of silence, this I figured would allow for the rumpus over Donald's demise and my well-acted bid to get the radio working.

"What you did was appalling, he didn't stand a chance, you saw the mess." Andrew raised his boot again, making Ian recoil in fear.

"As bad as cutting someone out of a life-changing sum of money while all the time talking about them behind their back? To carry on working with them as if nothing had happened? I never did anything to deserve that! I gather the plan was for you to put in for redundancy or slowly retire to avoid suspicion? You bunch of assholes had it all worked out, didn't you?" Ian shook his head frantically and pleaded for more time to explain.

"You've had enough time to explain, over three months' worth. So anyway, that more or less brings us up to date, obviously I spiked your drink after we had bravely decided to make a last stand in the living room, then waited for you to pass out. You've probably suffered liver damage because of that but I don't think it's going to bother you. While you were unconscious, I replaced the circuit boards in the radio, dismantled the shotgun and dumped them into the sea along with leftover sleeping pills, the faulty circuit boards, oh and not forgetting Donald and what was left of our much-vaunted supervisor. The living room is tidy again as is the kitchen, I also burnt those ridiculous statements he had us write out to save his career. It took over 40 minutes to clean the mess off the wall and trace all the left-over pellets - I was lucky none had hit the door frame!"

Andrew had reached the end of his explanation for murdering three people. The sky was darkening and icy rain was peppering the helipad. He knelt down to head height with Ian.

"Whose idea was it?"

Ian was shaking uncontrollably, he just repeated that they had all agreed on it purely on a silly remark Tony had made about having one less in the syndicate would have given them a much more extravagant lifestyle.

"Well Ian, I can't promise you an extravagant lifestyle but I can do the next best thing I'm sure"

"What do you mean, what do you mean?" came Ian's hysterical reply

"You will be the first person to fall backwards off Blade Rock lighthouse helipad while tied to a chair! How's that for extravagant? Before Ian could protest or plead again

Andrew savagely kicked the base of the chair sending it off the edge and plunging down alongside the granite wall accompanied by a horrific scream that even drowned out the wind briefly. A half splash half thud indicated Ian had reached journeys end. Andrew calmly looked down, the tempestuous white-water swirling around the base was turning crimson, the chair had broken apart leaving the crumpled body free to bob about wildly before being dashed against the rocks unceremoniously.

Andrew looked at his watch, it was now 8.15 am, by the time the supply helicopter arrived at 1 pm the world would be confronted with another baffling sea mystery to be recited for decades. He wasn't naive about modern-day forensics; they could well detect blood stains and pellet marks; detectives would poke about until they made the lottery connection. Bodies may well wash ashore, but for a few weeks he hoped this would be a mystery no one could solve.

The thundering black sky dwarfed Blade Rock lighthouse, the sea was once again starting its never-ending attack upon the rocks and base; the mournful howling wind again filled the air. Andrew stared out into the heart of the storm, nothing but endless grey and black clouds enveloped him. The revenge had been the only thing keeping him going. As with the fast approaching storm, so too with his life… endless blackness…

Blade Rock lighthouse, time 8.17am March 23, population 0.

Courtesy of the Local Gazette:

A lighthouse mystery to eclipse that of Flannan isle was discovered yesterday at the remote Blade Rock lighthouse off the Cornish coast. A regular supply helicopter arrived at 1 pm only to find the tower deserted. Five engineers had been dropped on the lighthouse the day before to carry out extensive work so that the light could be operated automatically. A spokesman for the company who own and operate the lighthouse gave the following account,

"It was reported that there were no signs of the five employees dropped on the lighthouse the day before, all rooms were in good order and both radio sets were fully functioning. The main doors were still sealed and no storm damage was evident." Commenting further on the men dropped at the tower, the spokesmen said it was clearly evident they had started work in one of the engine rooms and their personal belongings were neatly stowed in the bedroom.

Police will be liaising with the coast guard and a missing persons unit to solve the eerie mystery. A further statement will be issued in the next few days. The five missing men are:

Sam Brooks 61

Donald Woods 56

Andrew Seaton 42

Tony Carter 30

Ian Sanderson 36

LEAVE AT YOUR LEISURE

The lure of exploring a disused building captivates many of us. To reconnoitre every room, peel back the dust and decay trying to fathom out what took place and why…

The busier the building in its day the greater the feeling of loneliness that is left behind. One such abandoned building is lying in wait for a man on an arid day in June, he will enter full of idle curiosity and leave with doubts as to whether "seeing is believing."

May I ask you to please be gentle with the story you are about to read and treat it with an open mind? I know everyone has the right to deliberate, cogitate and pour scorn on what comes into his or her personal reading zone - but let me add that the story I am about to relate is perfectly true and recounted from the very best of my memory. I say MY memory because I was not told it second or third hand - I'm afraid to say that I was the miserable sport to the events you are about to be presented with. To this day they defy all my best efforts to even half explain them away in a pragmatic logical manner. So, with that said I will now let you be the judge...

It was June 2001, at the time I was employed as a telephone engineer and installation specialist, this took me over a wide area of the country, for which I was endlessly grateful, because it was quite a dreary job and I found myself enjoying the travelling much more than grubbing about running phone cables, testing internet signals or fault diagnostics.

I had unexpectedly been taken off a very monotonous installation job and told to make my way to the outskirts of Oswestry (not far from where I lived at the time). I would be given further instructions from my line supervisor in due course. I was as smug as a school boy who had managed to dodge a very unpleasant physical education class. I was packed up and on my way in no time. After 40 minutes or so the indistinct directions I had been issued with delivered me outside a long-abandoned fenced off leisure centre complex standing forlornly in a quiet defunct side road which was evidently due for redevelopment. Just as I was beginning to think I had been the recipient of an irritating faux pas my works mobile phone wheezed into life and my unbearable supervisor put me in the picture - so to speak.

I will do my best to condense the man's vexatious conversation. Even on my best day he had the unsurpassed ability to put me in a bad mood. It seemed there was quite a controversy raging over the derelict leisure centre.

On no less than four separate occasions hoax emergency calls had been traced back to one of the many landlines contained within the lonely complex. As you are no doubt aware these have to be taken seriously and the fire brigade were by now shouting rather loudly. Each time an exhaustive search of the building was carried out but always proved fruitless, the mystery caller or callers had long since scarpered.

The police had been brought in - who in turn scalded the private security firm and key holders to the building saying they were allowing trespassing. The security firm tried in vain to deflect some of the blame by accusing my company of not disconnecting all of the phone lines, as promised a few years ago. You know how the blame game always travels downwards.

I had been asked to attend the site to recheck and document that all phone lines were without any means of generating a call, thus removing our company from any blame in these dangerous hoaxes.

While waiting for the key holder and security representative for the building I ambled around the perimeter fence in the baking sunshine. In its day the centre would have been quite something and I will try and do it justice by describing it to the best of my ability.

The entrance block and right-hand section almost resembled a 1950's secondary school, neat red brick with generous sized metal frame windows. There was a large flat roofed porch jutting out from the building above the main entrance doors for seven or eight feet, supported by two metal poles. Above the porch was the year '*1957*' set into a circular stone. To the right the building ran for some distance in the form of a glass-panelled corridor before coming to a sheer face of windowless red bricks that rose some forty or more feet. The dimensions of this structure made it resemble a huge box. I took it to be squash courts or something similar.

The whole building was very much of two halves, with the left-hand side being all much later additions and bearing no resemblance to the original design and build - other than the glass-panelled corridor that again led off from the reception and entrance. Two towering ugly blue faded corrugated carbuncle structures then took complete dominance over anything else. They both had rows of narrow windows almost flush with the roof - many still wide open. They had to have once been an indoor swimming pool and sports hall, such was their size it was impossible to see what extended behind them. I would guess the whole site was over two acres, the ground surrounding the building was strewn with rubbish from fly-tippers, and in parts littered with the remnants of exterior fittings such as guttering, tiles and window frames. An outline of a medium-sized outdoor pool could be discerned close to the sharp pointed fencing on the right of the building, although this had been discourteously filled with rubble from a smaller structure that had evidently been demolished - perhaps it had been old changing rooms. All around weeds were pushing through the concrete and taking over.

I had become quite lost in surveying the fascinating building and hadn't noticed a small van pull up close to my own vehicle. In fact, the first I knew I had any company other than the row of curious Jackdaws that had been watching me from the rooftops, was of someone clearing their throat and introducing themselves.

"My name is Mr Blunt, I'm security for this site and the keyholder." I introduced myself and presented my works identification card which he examined for an inordinately long length of time in total silence. He then made his way over to a section of the fence that was festooned with a thick rusty chain on top of which lay a clamped padlock the size of a hand. As he wrestled with the chain and lock, I studied him in the brilliance of the light - he looked ridiculous. Easily six foot four but the long rubber mac he wore made him seem even taller. A hat clearly too small for him was perched on his head ready to pop off at any minute, his trousers where shiny black - I will use the term 'ankle flappers' and leave it at that, and to cap it all - he had kipper feet! I know I shouldn't comment on someone's appearance but he gave the unequivocal impression of having dressed like that for a bet.

"Right then this is the only way in through the fence, if you'd like to sign for the keys," he said firmly, still with his back to me. I jokingly asked if he was not coming in to show me around...

"I've 18 other sites all more important than this one under my jurisdiction, I don't have time to hang about here. That's the front door key and the other bunch will open anything else I suppose. I haven't been inside for a while - I guess it won't do any harm if you need to force open a door, it's being demolished sometime anyway," came the humourless reply. I then painfully managed to extract a few more details about the building of my new assignment. It had been called the "Valley Leisure and Fitness Centre." As the building's appearance suggested, it had started off with basic amenities and gradually grew with demand and it had enjoyed its boom time in the seventies and eighties. By the early 90's, due to its location and a much more modern user-friendly site having been constructed closer to town, it was relegated to a conference centre and private function rooms. Eventually even these scant duties proved insufficient to maintain its upkeep and it finally closed some five years ago.

Once inside the perimeter, Blunt handed me the grimy keys and his contact number and delivered another impromptu lecture.

"See that you call me when you want to leave, this place has caused enough bother without it being left unlocked, and I do have 20 other sites to attend to as well." I pointed out to him his sheer brilliance in gaining two more responsibilities in the last five minutes alone... He fixed me a look of undisguised disdain and promptly folded himself into his little van in true swiss army knife fashion and drove off leaving me alone outside the defunct building in the shimmering heat. Once Mr Personality was out of sight, I walked back to my company vehicle and collected all I would need for the task ahead, locked it and headed back to the sombre main entrance doors.

The wood and reinforced glass doors begrudgingly swung open - immediately my nose was accosted by the unmistakable odour of damp and decay. I locked the door behind me as a precaution to prevent anyone entering while I was engaged elsewhere. The foyer was a fair size - the glass corridors served to make it light and welcoming even in its terminal condition. Thieves had evidently started nibbling tentatively at the original parquet flooring leaving large ugly patches scattered about. Directly in front of me was an old-fashioned reception counter and behind that a door. On the far wall to the left of the counter was a row of six kiosk pay phones in varying states, while off to the right there were two doors side-by-side leading to male and female toilets and some chairs laid out in a large L shape. Just beyond these I could make out a wide staircase with a peeling utilitarian metal bannister.

The silence was unbroken in the dusty atmosphere as I made my way over to the reception counter and placed my tool box on its mouldering surface. I didn't know whether to start work or have a preliminary explore first. I opted to examine the row of ramshackle kiosk phones. Of the six, three were vandalized and missing their receivers but the other three had escaped the same brutal treatment. I removed the entire coin insert and push button casing from each of the kiosks and stacked them by the door. Having tested all the wiring, I then severed it as close to where it entered the wall as possible. There was no way any malicious calls could have come from these phones, they were long dead - but what the hell, I was just glad of the peace and quiet of the old place. I unscrewed the phone point at the reception desk and repeated this procedure in the little office behind it, then, tool box in hand, I set off down the right-hand corridor to start my surreptitious exploration.

Passing the stairs, I noticed a small wooden plaque fixed to the wall a few steps up with hand painted letters saying "Managers Office" and an old-fashioned caricature of a hand pointing upwards. Underneath this was another sign but of a totally maladroit effort and written on stiff cardboard in free hand - it read "Conference Rooms 1,2,3." Moving on and being watchful to avoid broken glass I arrived at a door on my left and stopped, the sun streamed through the pelted glass windows in the corridor and shone in my eyes. I could make out the austere fencing and my car beyond it in a heat haze. The door was locked but soon yielded to one of Mr Blunt's keys and I found myself in the one-time fitness room. The walls were still adorned with exercise charts and workout routines, a sort of rubberized matting covered the entire floor space and gave off a pungent unpleasant odour. In the far corner several large pieces of equipment such as treadmills and weight machines had evidently been deemed unworthy of removing when the building was abandoned and been left to deteriorate in situ.

Having seen enough I closed the door behind me and headed to the end of the corridor glad to be away from the miasma that lingered in the fitness room.

I had surmised correctly from my brief outside tour, that the large featureless walls rising up on the right side of the building were indeed squash courts. At the end of the corridor a door led to a changing room - still with its full complement of blue painted lockers many of which had their doors wide open as if waiting for a patron who would never show up. To the left there were showers and toilets which I had no interest in seeing so instead I headed through the only other door. I found myself in a sort of anti-room staring at two empty courts through a wall of Perspex. I entered Court One and walked to the far end, the white walls were littered with countless black marks from thousands of ball strikes. I had been wrong earlier, there were windows but not visible from the front of the building. A line of four rectangular windows were perched high up on the far wall of each court. Then came another discovery - I hadn't realised until I traced the peculiar zig zag shaft of light the windows afforded into the courts, that there was a viewing gallery for both playing areas above the door I had entered from. The empty court was getting calescent and held nothing more worth staying for so I decided to leave this wing of the complex.

At this point my day's adventure took its first unsettling turn. Standing as I was in the empty number one squash court; I had become intensely aware of the sensation of being watched from the dark recess of the viewing gallery. I had often heard people say they had the feeling of being watched but had never really paid it much heed. Well I can certainly vouch for that uncanny feeling now; the sensation was overwhelming and startling in its rapidness. The light from the queerly located windows did nothing to illuminate the gallery, as I stared up passed the safety rail and into the atramentous depths beyond, I became unnervingly convinced I was being studied by a person or persons unknown. The feeling grew and grew, any minute I expected to see someone or something step forwards out of the blackness and become visible to me…

This dreadful feeling was heightened by the sudden realisation which up until now I had foolishly not thought about. How did I know I was alone in the old place? A locked fence is easily scalable and from what I had seen of Mr Blunt it was obvious he had no interest in the building. By locking the front door had I not sealed myself in with squatters or something worse? I managed to pull myself out of these unhealthy conjectures and promptly left the humid squash court area and returned to the main corridor and staircase.

I ascended the stairs with mixed feelings, I was still curious in exploring the defunct leisure centre but the impression of being watched in the squash court had sullied my enthusiasm slightly, leaving me aware I could potentially be in a vulnerable situation. Reaching the top of the stairs was somewhat of an anti-climax, there was a short corridor with four doors leading off. The first door from the stairs had a round porthole style window in it and the sign on it confirmed it was the afore mentioned managers office. Three more doors opposite this were all open and without exception all empty. When examined each room was found to have a phone point which I again dealt with in short order. The little cubby hole of the manager's office still had a less than shoddy desk in place and I will ashamedly admit to looking through the drawers, however my inquisitive prying was suddenly halted...

From some unknown location I could hear a faint cry or whine... it was by no means blood curdling but more pitiful and wretched. I stood in perfect silence listening in the sweltering office, after a few more tormented moans it ceased. Then my senses made another discovery which I hadn't been aware of upon entering the diminutive office, the tiny confines seemed tainted with a rancid dense smell of smoke or burning. I disconnected the phone line and vacated the office only feeling more composed when I was back in the foyer and in sight of the entrance doors.

I left the building for a short while and sallied fourth to my car for a bottle of water. The brightness and heat were relentless, the tarmac felt malleable underfoot, and even the ubiquitous weeds and thorn bushes were wilting. I glanced back at the building and charted my progress so far; I had all but covered the whole right-hand portion. Then my eyes fixed upon the towering brickwork of the squash courts. Even in the full heat of the midday sun I felt a chill go up my sweat soaked back as I remembered that consuming feeling that I had been under observation from something unseen. I tried to flush the thoughts from my mind and with a good helping of mendacity I tricked myself into believing I had imagined the whole thing.

My thoughts then turned to my next conquest: the huge newer sections to the left-hand side. I once again headed into the tumbled down structure but this time deciding to leave the entrance doors wedged open with the aid of a few loose floor tiles. I kidded myself I had done this to get some air into the musty atmosphere but I'm sure you have deduced that subconsciously the open doors represented a more alacritous means of escape...

The left-hand corridor was in a far more neglected condition, large white ceiling tiles littered the floor - whether pulled down or just having come loose as the years of abandonment passed it was impossible to determine. An internal door had been ripped off its hinges and now lay propped up against a wall, a few paces further and the door frame it once hung on came into view. Judging from the metal racking I gathered the doorless room to have once been a caretaker's cupboard or supply room, an evil looking turquoise mould clung to the walls in flaking clumps. I pressed on to the ajar door at the end of the corridor gingerly poking my head round before entering it and leaving the bedraggled corridor behind. I found myself in a large changing room and shower area - much larger than the one that served the squash courts. Once again rows of featureless blue lockers stared back at me many having been the recipient of a sound beating. There were stout bench seats bolted to the floor at regular spacings - I counted five in total. The door which I exited from took me into a little white tiled corridor and I elected to follow the sign for the swimming pool first.

There is something pathetically dismal about an empty swimming pool - especially one that has long since seen water. I made my entrance from the shallow end and slowly walked around the vast blue tiled chasm, the floor was strewn with floatation aids and lane markers- now all useless. A dirty black patch at the deep end indicated where the last puddle of water had slowly evaporated - above this was perched a pink coloured diving board. There was little else to see in the long-forgotten natatorium except a tiny office marked 'Duty Life-Guard." I peered in and well near jumped out of my skin! I was face to face with a smooth featureless head turned in my direction! I stepped back instinctively and then at once the illusion was quickly broken. Some trespasser with a dry sense of humour had propped a first-aid dummy in an office chair to welcome the unwary. I regained my wits and quickly left the grotesque looking mannequin in peace. After walking all the way around the pool something caught my eye on the dusty bone-dry tiles. I climbed down and walked to about halfway and craned my head down and examined the floor. Freshly made foot prints had clearly traversed the dusty bed of tiles - coming from the deep end and leaving by the shallow. This would have not bothered me so much but for the clear undeniable fact these foot prints were made by someone walking barefoot…

As I was wrestling with this rather eldritch revelation the same mournful whimper from earlier came again carried on the warm summer air and found my ears. It somehow seemed closer but diminishing in stamina. I was certain that this place was (or had been) occupied and I would tell Blunt as much when he returned. Still clutching my tools, I left the deserted pool and headed back to the tiled corridor - I certainly had no wish to meet the owner of the bare feet who walked this place.

I found the door at the other end of the corridor locked so I once again enlisted the assistance of the master keys. The door opened revealing a very large sports hall, the wooden floor was covered with the usual myriad of lines and semi circles for various activities. At each end there was a basketball hoop jutting out from the wall on a metal bracket. To my right there was an alcove which I presumed would have been filled with equipment back in its hay-day, but sadly all that it contained now was a few slashed rubber crash mats, deflated footballs and crumpled cones. The furthest end of the hall probably invoked the saddest sight of all, there were about 50 green plastic chairs all facing an empty make shift stage. There is something universally eerie about rows of empty chairs and this proved no exception. The stage seemed set for a play of some kind, a large painted back drop was still in place depicting a grand sitting room - while in the centre was a table complete with place settings and elegant tall backed chairs. I walked to the stage softly to avoid making an echo, the suns white rays powered through the high windows and created a broken likeness of the frames on the walls and climbing bars opposite. Dust rose in lazily floating spirals amid the arid stillness, I stood in a cognitive mood on the dilapidated stage wondering how it came to pass that it could have been abandoned so hurriedly - it was like the absent audience had just this minute left the room…

At the moment I was shaken from my pointless

reasoning by an all too recognizable voice calling my name some way off and I wearily disembarked from the stage and left the scene of the unknown play.

"Oh, there you are, how's it going? I was passing and thought I'd look in." My ever 'helpful' supervisor was standing by the mouldy caretaker's cupboard. I gave him the best smile I could muster and reported that I had disconnected every landline I could find and was on the point of leaving.

"Ok that seems reasonable, can you call that security bloke to come and collect the keys?" He didn't wait for me to respond but instead wondered off into the changing rooms. I found Blunt's number and was told in a prickly tone he would be back in 30 minutes along with the now familiar clap-trap of how busy he was. At that point my Supervisor reappeared from the ajar door.

"No wonder this place went bust - the staff couldn't even layout chairs in the correct direction, I bet that play was a big success. Did you speak to him? When is he coming down?" I informed him of Blunts estimated time of arrival and asked if he wanted to wait for him.

"No that's ok you stay here; I can't hang about waiting on him. You being here is absolutely pointless anyway, the phone wires coming into the building were disconnected years ago - this is a paper exercise to shut people up."

"If that was the case (and I had no doubt it was) then how were the calls being made?"

"No idea, they obviously don't know much about phone

lines - the theory is one of the points here is still connected, absolute rubbish."

"But who would be in here and why?" I said in an agitated tone.

"Don't know don't care, it's probably a mistake anyway, right I'll see you tomorrow back on site, if he's longer than half an hour you lock up and he will have to collect the keys from us." This man had the unsurpassed talent to irritate me even in the smallest of doses.

"Yeah see you tomorrow," I feebly replied - I don't think he could have heard me as he was already past the gap in the fence. I walked back once more to the reception desk and gave one final glance around the place, there was a certain something about this whole set-up that made me want to find out more. I walked to the main door and started kicking my make shift door wedges away - then suddenly stopped…

"Chairs facing the wrong direction… what did he mean by that?" I said out loud… I left the wedges in place and headed back down the left-hand corridor in a hurried state, any slight fears being smothered by burning inquisitiveness. I was through the changing room and tiled corridor in a few seconds and then outside the sports hall door. Without pausing I opened the door and in my best mettlesome demeanour strode into the vastness…

It was how I had feared it would be… without any exception every one of the green chairs was now facing away from the stage and in my direction. The hairs on my damp neck started to rise…this couldn't be possible but it was. The rows still retained their uniformed layout and neatness but were bereft of any tell-tale sweaty hand prints adorning their dusty backs. I glanced around the hall expecting any minute to lay eyes on the perpetrator of this impossible feat of dexterity but no such being came in reply to my gaze. Someone or something still inhabited this doomed building and perhaps ambled round on some infernal night skulduggery making phone calls from long dead phone lines… Goosebumps and a growing uneasiness told me it was time to leave this building and be thankful I hadn't been subjected to anymore oddities.

For the first time that day the oppressive radiating heat and hot summer air were a welcome. I perched myself on the warmth of my cars front wing and stared away from the melancholy building in a trance. Was I sure all the chairs were facing the stage on my first inspection? I hadn't been long enough away from the room for it to be possible for all of them to be turned around - even allowing for my brief chat in the corridor, my supervisor... what of him? A practical joke? Impossible for two reasons: 1 - he had no sense of humour and 2 - he hadn't been gone long enough. I flung both doors open and sat inside my car feeling fatigued, I still had some 25 minutes before "Happy" turned up and they were dragging. I tried in vain to distract myself with the radio and nibbling at a rapidly curling sandwich but my mind was elsewhere…

"You bloody fool" I cursed out loud as I retraced my steps in the building, somewhere on my travels I had dropped my voltage reader! It would have to be the most expensive single item from my tool kit. I searched the reception area and then suddenly remembered climbing down into the pool, it must have dropped out then. I shuddered at the thought of the barefooted wonderer but even that was preferable to the unknown presence in the squash court. I hastily paced the tiles searching… it was very rash of me not to pay more attention to my surroundings… I was in the deep end when I glanced up… the grotesque faceless first-aid mannequin had now travelled from the office to a slouched loll on the quivering diving board… terror gripped me and I at once elected to leave. I followed the horrid footprints for what seemed an age but I made little progress in any direction! The side of the pool didn't get any closer - I was dripping with sweat and confused, trapped like a spider in a glass. Finally exhausted I slumped onto the tiled floor underneath the occupied diving board. Over the sound of my own panting came a 'tramp, tramp, tramp' the producer of the footprints had returned. I couldn't move… my limbs were set fast and useless.

Slowly, very slowly, the feeling of being watched took sure but steady possession of me, in my mind's eye I could see a tumbling black mass rolling down the corridor heading to where I lay stranded, the footsteps continued their troop. I could see something entering the far door, I collapsed on my back in paralysis - glancing up at the gently rocking diving board, I cried out as the mannequin was now staring directly at me with freshly acquired black sunken eyes and a fixed flagitious grin….

I woke with a start, sweating profusely my shirt stuck to

my back. The sun pitched in through the passenger's side open window burning my face. I glanced down at my tool box on the vacant seat and breathed a sigh of relief as I noticed my voltage meter was safely onboard.

"Jesus what a crazy dream," I murmured in a breathless debilitated tone. I gathered my senses and looked at my watch - I had been asleep some 15 minutes. Somehow the recent strange events I had stumbled upon in the forlorn leisure centre had become jumbled up in my over active brain to produce a truly frightening nightmare. With only a few minutes to go before Blunt turned up, I exited the car feeling harassed and nervous and stretched my legs around the weed infested perimeter fence. I hadn't gone very far when yet again that mournful whimpering lamentation came again on the wind. It seemed to be coming from outside and if I wasn't mistaken close to the indoor pool. This was one secret this anomalous site wasn't going to hold onto and take with it into its demolition. Hurrying before the wailing stopped, I set out to find the perpetrator of this sorrowful croon…

Trampling down tall weeds and thickets I picked up on the remnants of a path leading through swathes of stinging nettles. I followed it until it took me to the very rear of the indoor pool section. I fixed my position with a set of wide fire doors I had noticed when inside. Sporadic gatherings of bricks lay all about, interspersed among these were rusty oil barrels, rotting timbers and general rubbish. By now the crying had stopped, I was annoyingly none the wiser for my journey. I stood listening to the quarrelling Jackdaws on the roof above me, the huge structure around me and that of the sports hall further on served to give this area an enclosed sun trap feel. The towering walls also stopping any slight relief from the breeze reaching me. I was on the point of leaving when a noticeable larger mound of bricks and rubble caught my attention, two large wooden beams protruded from it partially covered with a lacerated blue tarpaulin. I judiciously approached the mound my heart was beating hard, I took a deep breath and hurled back the tarpaulin…

A pair of frightened watery brown eyes and a podgy black and white snout stared up at me from almost between my dusty shoes and remained fixed, pointed ears were angled towards me like radar dishes. The terrified collie puppy I discovered tied to a metal spike couldn't have been more than two months old, I bent down and offered my hand to him. Despite all he had been subjected to, the little fellow greeted me as best his depleted energy allowed and wagged his matted tail. I quickly checked the entire area to make sure another poor wretch wasn't also suffering a similar fate and then returned to the ailing pup. Undoing the metal clip on the chain I gently scooped him up. I half expected to be bitten out of the poor things distrust and terror, he had every right to, was it not another of my kind who had pegged him out to a lonely death here in this awful place… The little pup nuzzled into my arms as I hurried him away to my car. At first, he had to be coaxed as if wary but then he drank my bottled water furiously and quickly devoured the rest of my sandwiches.

"What you found there then? Made a new friend, have we?" I looked round to see the beanpole stature of Blunt leaning up against the car with his sticky looking mac flapping in the breeze. I was in a splenetic mood and fixed him a fuming look.

"What's it look like? I just found him behind the swimming pool building, looks like he's been there a few days. Oh, but wait he can't have been can he - because your company is supposed to be checking around the building regularly…. I was forgetting this isn't one of your important sites is it...?" Before Blunt could reply I tossed the keys back at him.

"Your keys - it will need locking. All the works completed. Goodbye." I closed both the doors and secured the little pup on the passenger seat with an old jumper as a bed.

"Aren't you coming around with me inside then? Now you have been all through it, I will have to go around and check every door, it's policy."

"No, I've done my job I have a more important site to visit. Oh I think the window in the little office by the swimming pool will need closing." I patted the resting pup and drove off with a chuckle at the thought of Blunt coming face to face with the creepy mannequin as I had done.

…….

I have a new friend who accompanies me on my travels now, after two nights recuperation and care at the nearest veterinary surgery the little pup I rescued was fighting fit and I immediately adopted him. Never one to be good with names I christened him 'Blaze'- owing to the weather conditions when I discovered him. He's a cheeky little fellow who never ceases to brighten my day. He also serves as a permanent reminder of my perplexing visit to the disused leisure centre which has now long since gone and some remarkable events which I still mull over now and then…

"An enigma laying abandoned in the midday sun… corridors without hustle, a swimming pool without water, chairs set for a play that will never resume and phone calls made from lines that no longer exist… Funny how your mind can trick you into believing the impossible… or is it simply showing you what's credible?"

THE INHERITANCE

They say the road to hell is paved with good intentions or no good deed goes unpunished... Loner Emma Maynard is about to find out these timely old phrases can ring true. An act of benevolence from a long forgotten relative is about to demonstrate this in terrifying clarity. The greater the act of kindness the darker the evil that can follow it...

...."May I offer you my deepest condolences Miss Maynard regarding the rather sad and untimely passing of your uncle?" said sombre faced Mr Osborne of Osborne, Osborne and Clark.

"Please call me Emma, it's rather awkward all this, but the truth is... I only met my uncle once when I was a child. I don't even know where he lives - sorry I mean lived."

"There's no need to feel embarrassed Miss Maynard, in my profession, I deal with this sort of situation on a fairly regular basis, a long lost or out of touch relative leaving a bequest to another family member is more common than you think." Emma Maynard nervously raised her right hand and tucked a length of her straight black shoulder-length hair behind her ear.

"Your letter said about being bequeathed something? I'm quite sure it is a mistake if you..." Mr Osborne diplomatically interrupted.

"It is my instructed duty to inform you, Miss Maynard, that you are the chief beneficiary in your late uncle's will, one might almost say the sole beneficiary. There are some small bequests to members of staff and a district nurse.

"Sorry did you say, staff? Did my uncle have his own business then?" Mr Osborne stifled a frown and placed down his papers on a green leather inlaid writing desk.

"I can see you were not exaggerating your un-enlightenment regarding your late uncle's whereabouts and situation. Your uncle had lived for the last 27 years in Yorkshire, he had no business interests as far as we can ascertain. The staff to whom I referred to earlier reside on his estate." Mr Osborne paused briefly to pick up his notes, he then turned two pages and ran his finger down a sheet of pristine white paper to about halfway.

"Your inheritance Miss Maynard is your late uncle's entire country estate, this consists of a grade two listed 10-bedroom Georgian house, freehold of course. All the land he owned without exception - 95 acres in total, parkland, a lake, a small working farm etc. There are also stable blocks and three cottages that are let privately. You will find all the details in this pack; I understand it is a lot to take in but please read it all carefully and remember we are to offer any assistance you may require. Mr Clark will contact you in a few days, he deals with the financial side of things." Emma hadn't moved an inch since Osborne had explained the reason for her summoning to the antiquated office. She politely asked for a glass of water and after a few timid sips, asked "Financial side of things?"

Mr Osborne was collating the papers and putting them all into a stiff cream coloured folder, he answered only when he had finished.

"Yes Miss Maynard, all your late uncles' bank accounts, bonds and sources of income, you are now in possession of them. I suggest next week you visit your estate and introduce yourself; you will need to determine if you intend to reside there permanently or dispose of some, or all of the estate…you must remember you now have considerable means and must consider your options wisely."

A bitterly cold February wind buffeted Emma's small car as she anxiously got within a few miles of her uncle's house. She scalded herself twice over... and remembered it's not his house anymore it was hers and everyone referred to it as an estate! The drive up had been gruelling, she was fatigued and edgy. Wintery showers lashed the car at random intervals, the never-ending country roads all seemed alike. The wrong turns and irksome map reading had depleted her energy, but at the end of this peregrination, she still had to arrive at whatever it was called... something manor and introduce herself!

"This is ridiculous, what do I say? Hello, I'm your new employer I'm here to see if I want to sack you all and sell the land," she said out loud while adjusting the windscreen wipers to cope with a new barrage of icy rain that was once again sweeping the landscape.

Emma was 39, single with no children - her last relationship had been abusive and she was happy to be on her own now. A handful of days ago she was living in a one-bedroom flat near Swindon, locked in mortal battle with the Job Centre about benefits - yet now she was in an alien part of the country driving to some stuffy mansion after being reservedly told she was the new owner of a vast estate. The wintery showers increased and before long the frigid air was teaming with snowflakes. Emma once again pulled off the road to seek counsel with her tattered map. Tracing the road with her finger in weary frustration she idly threw a glance to her right and noticed two large grey square stone pillars with bulbous granite spheres at their summit some 50 feet away. The afternoon light was growing feeble while overhead the falling snow was increasing, selecting first gear the car doddered up the road the short distance and stopped alongside the two imposing monoliths. There was a large slate sign fixed to the left-hand pillar which read "*Marsden Manor*" then underneath this was a smaller sign which read *"private"*. Emma fumbled through her handwritten instructions that were laying open on the map book... Yes, this was the place... she felt a slight sickness wash over her as she crossed the threshold...

So engrossed had she been in reading the sign, a medium-sized gatehouse had escaped her notice some 40 or so feet further down nestling sedately behind some tall trees. Smoke poured from the solitary chimney and was quickly dispersed on the raw wind. A light burned from a window facing her and looked welcoming in the fading light. She slowly crossed over a cattle grid and then stopped outside the homespun little dwelling. Grabbing her body warmer from the backseat she left her car and headed to the yellow-painted door, passing the lit-up window as she went. She respectfully knocked on the door and waited...no one came, so she increased her rap and supplemented it with a prosaic "hello". Again no one came in answer to her arrival and call.

Emma felt awkward and slightly embarrassed and thought things over quickly. "Can I just walk in? Should I look through the window? Someone must be here... Not wanting to wait any longer or disturb anyone she got back into her car and decided to head towards the main house which was ill-defined in the flat grey light and swirling snow storm.

The single-track panoramic drive was flanked on both sides by large open parkland quickly becoming blanketed in a brilliant sheen from the wintery sky. At random points, massive gaunt oak trees towered upwards giving the unflawed impression of noble grandeur. Then further on after a slight curve, the house came squarely into view and commanded her attention. It would be doing the building a huge injustice calling it a "house". The mansion with its snow-covered roof and numerous bulky chimney stacks were Georgian and dated from 1815. It was perfectly square with an elegant uncluttered symmetrical facade. The first and second floor each had four rows of large original sash windows while an impressive portico entrance on the ground floor took the place of the two middle windows leaving one at each end. The roof was typically of a shallow pitch but with wide overhangs. A row of stables built in an L shape sat to the left of the mansion some 50 yards distant while to the right an octagonal dovecot stood gaunt against the storm. Emma surmised she should be feeling excited or lucky but the sheer scale of the property was daunting. She found it impossible to comprehend that ever since she turned off the country lane and passed the stone pillars, everything she had seen was hers…

Pulling up outside the grand entrance she composed herself, taking a deep breath before leaving her car. The snow had increased and she had to wipe it off the boot lid before being able to find the lock to retrieve her small scruffy holdall. A quick dash and she was out of the falling snow and under the protection of the beautiful marble porch. Before her confidence could ebb, she loudly gave three knocks on the hefty door knocker. A faint female voice from within responded to the knocks,

"Come in please, it's open." Emma did as the disembodied voice asked and turned the ice-cold brass door handle and pushed open the door. There was nobody on the other side to greet her just a black and white tiled corridor which ran some way then led into a large open reception hall with a breath-taking central staircase that rose eight or nine steps before elegantly branching off to the left and right, the entire length of which was bordered by a dark wooden bannister handrail held in place by dignified twisting spindles. Stopping at the foot of the stairs Emma called out in a welcoming tone,

"Hello, you said come in, my name is Emma." Suddenly she felt awkward again, her dark shiny shoulder-length hair was flecked with snow and her blue jeans looked scruffy.

"Good afternoon my dear," came a voice off to her left. She jumped and dropped her holdall onto the lustrous tiles. A square-framed woman in her early 50's appeared from a door and walked towards her with a salubrious smile.

"My name is Mrs Dobbs but please call me Pam, you must be Emma Maynard we know all about you coming - the solicitor told us."

Emma cleared her throat, "Hi Mrs... I mean Pam, I'm sorry I didn't know if I should have waited at the gatehouse building - I did knock but there was no reply. You made me jump". She could sense herself getting flustered and felt foolish.

"No, my dear please don't worry it's entirely my fault. Me and my husband Frank live in the gatehouse we should have been there to welcome you to your new home but when this snow started, we both dashed up here quick to light a few of the fires and sort the central heating out. A home this size takes hours to heat. The last thing we wanted was to welcome you to lots of freezing cold rooms. Now don't you worry my dear me, and my Frank have only been here 20 odd years, we are originally from London so I'm not going to go all yokel on you." Emma felt relieved, the friendly welcome had been just what she needed and some of the tension left her. Pam told her to leave her bag where it was for the time being and come through to the kitchen for a cup of tea. She explained that Frank was upstairs airing rooms and would be down in a little while, and then she would show her around.

Keeping to the left of the reception hall they passed the stairs and then turned into the room where Pam had first appeared from. It was a sizeable wood-panelled dining room which extended back towards the direction of the entrance doors. The kitchen flowed off of this, opening up before them as they carried on straight.

"Here we are dear please have a seat," Pam said while motioning with an attentive gesture to an enormous solid kitchen table that was loaded with cake stands and plates of sandwiches. The kitchen was very probably the size of Emma's entire flat. She sat with her back to the door, to her left a huge inglenook fireplace crackled away chucking its warmth around the sprawling room, to her right were a ramshackle collection of substantial units and two large Butler sinks, then came the amplest Aga cooking range she had ever seen, it was easily as long as her car! A large pipe extended upwards from the middle of this shiny black iron monster and out the wall at about halfway before the ceiling. A multitude of pots, pans and utensils hung around the room, past the slumbering Aga there were two latched doors leading to a utility room on the left and the other was a large walk-in pantry.

After a brief silence, Pam poured out two cups of steaming tea from a portly brown teapot, as she did so she implored Emma to help herself to scones and sandwiches. Emma once again felt a discomfiture digging away at her and nervously gave Pam a brief account of her situation and the shock of the whole thing. For some reason, Emma felt like some sort of scrounger who had turned up to pick over the bones of her late uncle's affairs.

"Now you stop that sort of talk Emma, your uncle was of a perfectly sound mind he left you all this because that was what he wanted." Emma tried to counter this comment with the contemptable fact that she had only met her uncle once in his entire life. She hadn't even been that close to her late father!

Pam sipped her tea and soothingly said, "People lose

touch, time passes then after so much has elapsed it seems ridiculous to establish contact again. Morris - your uncle was a kind and respectful employer he just wanted everything he had worked for to go to his only remaining relative." Emma nodded in a doleful mood. Pam then explained that she was the housekeeper and her husband was a general handyman. They had lived in the gatehouse ever since coming to work on the estate. Mr Grimes was the estate manager he had the largest cottage on the land and the furthest away from the main house, another cottage a few hundred yards from the stable block was rented by a Mrs Heathcoat - she operated a part-time riding school from the stables and used several of the paddocks. The other cottage was now and then used as a holiday let but at present was vacant.

Just then, a not so tall stocky bearded man entered the room from the utility room door and set about brushing the snow off his coat and stamping his shoes on the coconut mat.

"Frank, come on in and meet Emma Maynard she's not long got here." Frank Dobbs beamed a great smile and shook Emma's hand. He apologised for the delay and explained he had been out to the coal shed and brought fresh supplies in for the night. His eyes then lit up at the range of delicacies on the table.

"Right let's all get stuck in; come on Emma you're not eating - try the sandwiches everything is locally sourced." The three of them chatted away for several hours in the warm kitchen, swapping stories and life experiences while outside in the blackness the snow continued to silently fall. Eventually Pam rose from the table and glanced at the grimy face of the antique wall clock that hung over the white sinks.

"Frank, we have kept Emma far too long; I'll show her around while you start locking up. Sorry dear, I totally forgot about your long journey up here." Frank reluctantly bid Emma goodnight and disappeared into the gloom of the dining room.

Pam once again led the way and together the two of them toured the chilly greyness of the entire building. The layout of Marsden Manor was thus:

The ground floor consisted of an entrance corridor, reception hall, with a large sitting room to the left and drawing room to the right - both these rooms had one front-facing window as they were in between the portico. Further on past the drawing-room there was a study, which could be accessed independently or through an adjoining door in the drawing-room. Further past the sitting room was the already mentioned dining room which of course led onto the kitchen. There was a cloakroom tucked away before the kitchen and another in the utility room.

First floor: Five bedrooms on this level, three of which being en-suite with the principal bedroom also having a large dressing room running off it. To the right of the stairs was a large communal bathroom and tucked away discreetly beyond that were the one-time servants' stairs.

Second floor: Four bedrooms, this time all were en-suite and one contained a fully fitted kitchen thus making it a self-contained flat or granny annexe. The final room on this level was now empty but Pam said it was once a games room and use to boast a snooker table and bar area. Also running off the landing there was of course, more servants' stairs.

They eventually arrived back on the spacious first-floor landing, Emma had enjoyed the tour but the house seemed cold and offered little to welcome a stranger.

"We've put you in this one Emma above the sitting room, it's a lovely room and cheerful in the mornings. Frank has made the fire up and the radiator should be getting warm soon - they take a while the Aga isn't as young as it once was." Emma felt lost as she entered the large bedchamber and glanced around sheepishly. A bed of glowing coal radiated from a little green tiled fireplace in the corner.

"There are fresh towels in the bathroom dear and the water will be nice and hot shortly, now I better just give you your own set of keys… well, to be honest, they were your uncles. I won't go through them all now, just the basics". Emma felt it was almost symbolic being handed the late owners keys. Pam's tone had now noticeably changed slightly to that of an oration. She clearly informed her where all of the phones were in the house (only three in total) pressing zero would get her directly through to the gatehouse. Frank's brought your bag up dear, it's on the bed. Emma followed Pam out onto the landing almost akin to a frightened puppy following someone it trusted, not wanting them to leave.

"Pam, did my uncle stay here every night on his own? I didn't say earlier but the one time I met him was at my auntie's funeral - I can't have been more than nine or ten. He never remarried or anything?"

"No dear he never had any other love interests, not since me and Frank have known him. A couple of times a year he would hold a few large social gatherings but not for the last three of four years owing to his health. I think he quite liked the loneliness here".

"Can I ask… well without being disrespectful, what did he die of, I mean from? Sorry if that sounds tawdry".

"It's ok dear you don't need to stand on ceremony with me or Frank. Your uncle took a nasty tumble down the servants' stairs. He often used them at night if he wanted to make himself a cup of tea as they lead out into the utility room. Frank found him in the morning, shook him up something awful. Anyway, they did all the post… err whatever you call them and it showed he died instantly. He must have been frailer than we thought. Mr Grimes wanted him to move into the vacant cottage but Morris would hear none of it. He loved this big old house." Emma felt another wave of anxiety envelope her and wished she hadn't asked.

When kindly Pam Dobbs finally said goodnight and left the mansion by the front door to make her way back to the distant gatehouse which was now festooned with drifting snow, she took with her a precious commodity… sound. Emma stood in the chilly hall corridor watching Pam's trudging progress taking her further away and leaving her feeling more isolated.

The senile rhythmic ticking of a ginormous grandfather clock in the cavernous reception hall and the far-off spitting of the kitchen fireplace were the only things left for company. Emma bounded up the stairs and branched off left, her only thoughts were to lock herself in and leave in the morning. She quickly opened her door and bounded in backwards and span round, but wait. The room was now cold and dark. She fumbled for the light switch and eventually found it, what a fool she felt! This wasn't her room at all! In her haste to climb the stairs, she had turned to the left which had brought her out at the wrong end of the landing in relation to the room she was billeted in and almost reversed the layout.

The room Emma had unwittingly stumbled into was easily half as big again as her own. Two huge sash windows commanded a view over the front of the house and beyond. In the far corner two closed doors stared back at her while in the other corner there was a large fireplace with beautifully decorated tiles and glossy black hearth. Close to the fire was the biggest four-poster bed she thought imaginable. Thick satin embroidered green curtains were neatly tied back in each corner with a silver cord, each of the posts was a foot thick and teamed with beautiful carvings of entwined ivy. Two opulent dark red Persian rugs covered the floor, upon those she counted no less than six dark brown leather fireside chairs, several occasional tables and two inlaid rosewood jardinières scattered about. Emma walked a few steps more into the room, immediately on her right she saw an impressive walnut writing bureau with barley twist legs, tucked up close to it was a solid high-backed oak chair. Suddenly she realised this must have been her late uncles' room... Pam had just referred to it as the "principal bedroom" during her tour. Immediately Emma felt like an intruder and exited the room. Closing the door behind her then heading back to the staircase and finding her room, the glow and warmth from the little fire brought some comfort and reassurance.

After a bath and making up the fire Emma got into the lumbering old bed, it had been a bizarre day and she felt overwhelmingly tired. She lay back on the plump pillows trying to take it all in. She just felt like a guest here not the new owner, it was as if she should have breakfast in the morning thank the Dobbs for their hospitality and leave. None of it felt right, she decided to opt for the cowardly way out and hand the whole thing over to the solicitors.

Emma woke with a start, confused at first by her new surroundings she felt for her bedside lamp. Then it dawned on her where she was and she reached over to the other side of the bed and switched on the little lamp with its pink frilly shade. Looking at her mobile phone it was a little after 2 am. Another isolating wave hit her; the top of the phone displayed the depressing message "no service." The lamp did little to light the room, all four corners remained bathed in blackness. She could just make out the door to the en-suite bathroom and a green chair with her clothes on. Knowing further sleep was out of the question she tip-toed over to the chair and quickly dressed, then added more coal to the fire which eagerly came back to life. Looking outside the pale light was just sufficient to make her aware that the snow had stopped, but the landscape was covered. She sighed, thinking this might delay her departure tomorrow. Suddenly she felt an overwhelming hunger and remembered she had hardly eaten anything on her arrival, due to the anxiety and trying to come to terms with her surroundings. Switching her phone to torch mode she decided to steal down to the kitchen and bring back a few of the passed over items from earlier.

The dark landing and chill that greeted her were demoralizing and served almost to send her scurrying back into her room like a frightened mouse. She elected to only use the light from her phone to guide her, she had no intention to start groping round the walls for switches. She was almost at the main staircase when she remembered what Pam had said about the servant's stairs leading directly into the utility room and headed over to them. The stairs themselves were extremely steep, straight and devoid of carpet, going slowly she was almost at the bottom, when it struck her this is where the awful end of her uncle had come about. An iciness made her shudder at the thought and she speedily opened the latched door at the bottom and entered the utility room.

The huge shadowy cooking range greeted her with ticking and creaking, the once cheery fire was now a dull glow. Selecting a plate from a dish rack close to the sink Emma made her selections from the now covered food, some scones, two sandwiches and a glass of milk. Not wanting to use the calamitous servants' stairs again she headed out past the dining room and into the numbing reception hall. Before ascending the stairs, she became aware of a faint "tap, tap, tap." Resting her glass and plate down on the bottom step she listened in a state of agitated nervousness... It wasn't the grandfather clock which was still ticking, as it had probably always done for decades - these sounds came from one of the front rooms she narrowed it down to the sitting room. In a mood which could only be described as pusillanimous, Emma pushed open the door and stared into the blackened room... The solitary sash window was gently being buffeted by the gelid wind outside producing the eerie tapping noise. She didn't enter the room but instead collected her foraged snack and retreated from the cold darkness of the echoing hall and the collection of friendless rooms that fed off it.

Restlessly Emma picked over the food, then remembering the folder that Mr Osborne had left with her she retrieved it from her holdall and flicked through various documents in a phlegmatic manner. She was on the point of casting them to one side when a tiny envelope fell out onto the bedclothes. It had evidently been folded back behind a bigger document. She delicately opened it and held it closer to the lamp. It read:

I am hoping this note finds you well Emma,
No doubt you are feeling a little overwhelmed,
My house and everything in it are now yours,
Your new future starts here, so take your time,
Stay as long as you like, like what you stay for,
Try to forgive me for not contacting you sooner,
Underlying health issues have made me weak,
Do administer your new-found wealth wisely,
You will find it opens up all manner of opportunities,

Living here can be lonely but I hope you will stay,
Accept help from my solicitors but be wary of others,
Keenness to rush in could spell danger or worse,
Every day that passes will make you stronger,

Emma felt crestfallen, not only was the note poorly worded and agonisingly short. It armed her with nothing useful in regards to dealing with the running or administration of the estate. She folded the little note into a quarter and put it in her jeans pocket. She turned off the light and waited for the morning so that she could leave this place and not return.

Waking late Emma hurried downstairs, the tiles were cold on her socked feet.

"Morning Emma, breakfast in five minutes - bacon and eggs," came Pam's voice from the hazy depths of the kitchen. While she waited Emma nervously paced the grand hall, not wanting to chat to Pam out of a sense of guilt over her planned departure. Walking to the right she opened the far door and impatiently paced in. A large well-appointed study greeted her. A pale winter sun meekly entered the rear-facing windows and did its best to cheer this most imposing of rooms. The walls were dark red and adorned with many original paintings and giltwood mirrors. Three dark green Chesterfield sofas were neatly arranged around a Victorian walnut card table, towering mahogany bookcases lined the left-hand wall spaced neatly between two Sheraton revival satinwood desks. In front of the windows sat a heavily carved 19th-century oak kneehole twin pedestal writing desk and behind that a captain's office swivel chair finished in oxblood leather.

Emma glanced at the desk and counted eleven draws each with beautiful brass handles, it was almost as if she were expected to sit down and take up the reigns and start making decisions. This idea disheartened her and she was happy to be distracted by three impressively sized model ships surrounded by protective glass cases in the far corner just past another superlative tiled fireplace. The models were sat on a large high beech wood table with stout legs that ended in huge lions' feet that seem to dig into the thick carpet. The model which was the largest and most prominently displayed was that of an old cargo vessel called the *"Commissioner-General."* A study of the paintings on the wall was cut short by Pam's arrival and the announcement breakfast was ready.

Although hungry, Emma picked hesitantly at her food, trying to work out the best time to announce she was leaving. However, any such decision was quickly curtailed by Pam as she poured the tea.

"The roads are blocked leading to town; Frank has gone to see how bad it is. It should clear in a day or two, that's the trouble not being on a well-used road." Emma felt queasy at the thought of another day or two here. She sipped at her tea and tried to remain calm. Sensing that Pam was picking up on her lack of ebullience she unpremeditatedly blurted out -

"Can I borrow some boots or wellies, Pam? It would be great to look over everything." Pam seemed delighted with this idea and assured her she could kit her out for the longest of treks. Emma thanked her and then asked Pam what her late uncle did for a living and how he maintained the house and grounds.

"I thought you might ask that dear - to be honest with you, me and Frank don't really know and we are not people to pry. I can tell you that Morris bless him never once forgot to pay our wages and we got a bonus at Christmas - not to mention what he left us in the will." She then assumed a more serious tone, as before when handing over the keys.

"Emma you might hear gossip about your uncle having money or something stashed, it's all rubbish. For as long as we have worked here the villagers have teased us asking if we have found the misers hoard yet – it's all rot dear."

Emma thought things over for a bit and suddenly realised the more she discovered about her uncle the less she knew…

Fully kitted out with wellies, woolly hat and a coat at least two times too big for her, Emma set out from the utility room door with Pam's copious directions emblazoned on her mind.

Footprints aplenty were evident around the stable block; she couldn't tell how many occupants the building housed but one equine resident seemed particularly highly-strung, snorting and kicking the door so she carried on round to the rear of the house. Invisible to her from her window last night was a long narrow red-tiled roofed garage or carport. There were four vehicles parked neatly in their designated spaces. Emma had very little interest in cars but she did find herself studying them with interest. Two Range Rovers - both black with cream leather interiors, then a silver Mercedes with heavily tinted windows and finally a very long green jaguar. So long in fact, it stuck out by a foot from the protection of the roof. She wondered if this was a converted coach house or something - the wooden beams above each space and vertical supports seemed ancient. The drifting snow had blown in overnight giving the floor a frosted cake appearance. Leaving the silent machines to their slumber, Emma headed across the parkland and fields.

The progress was hard going, in places the snow reached to her knees. The whiteness had made everything featureless – pretty, but featureless. Following a skeletal hedge line for some 10 minutes, it suddenly banked to the right and a prodigious sized lake came into view. The water took on an intensely cerulean colour against the pure white snow that surrounded it. Emma stared out at the icy water thinking how odd it was, she now owned a lake! Not a run of the mill lake either, this one boasted a central island! No more than 40 feet square, a densely vegetated islet sat serenely - it's only inhabitants' birds. It looked like, at one point in its past, someone had regularly visited it. There was a good-sized landing stage but curiously, a structure was just visible in the midst of two trees and chaotic foliage. In the summer no evidence of its existence would be visible - Emma wondered what it could be.

She followed the contours of the shoreline until coming to a squat thatched roof structure almost dug into the bank. It was open-ended and peering into it, revealed it to be a boathouse. A well-built glossy white rowing boat was secured to an iron post inside, with two oars propped up against the corner alongside. If it had been a brilliant summer day, she could well have been tempted to take the boat out. It had been years since she used a rowing boat but she expected it was like riding a bike – you never forget.

Leaving the peaceful lake, Emma clumsily walked on further over a few more fields until a pale-yellow cottage came into view. Underneath its temporary snow cap a thatched roof could be seen. It was a long but well-shaped cottage with three windows on either side of a beautiful solid white door. Emma was enchanted and followed the picket fence until she came to a gate baring the rustic log sign *"Orchard cottage"*. The name instantly seemed familiar and feeling in the bottomless pockets of the big coat, she eventually pulled out her newly acquired keys and flicked through the tags. There was a tag marked with the same name - it must be the vacant cottage that was sometimes used as a holiday let. Without a second thought, Emma opened the gate and was almost at the welcoming door when a voice called out…

"Do you mind telling me what you're doing?"

Emma dropped the keys and span round to see a square-jawed man wearing a green waxed jacket and tatty cap pulled down low glaring at her. She felt frightened but was determined to brazen it out.

"Well actually I was just going to look around my cottage, in fact - may I ask what you think you're doing?

This is my land". This response had its desired effect and the man immediately assumed a more friendly line of questioning.

"Sorry, you seem to have the advantage of me? My name is Mr Grimes - I'm the estate manager here. I've not seen you before and as the cottage is unoccupied, I couldn't be sure who you were. You said you own it - you must be Morris's niece then?"

Emma introduced herself and gave Mr Grimes precious little else. He asked if she wanted to still see inside the cottage but she elected to save it for another day when she was alone. Mr Grimes said he would need to visit the stable block shortly and asked if she was heading back to the house. Not wanting to be trudging through the snow making awkward conversation she said she wasn't sure yet and quickly changed the subject.

"I've not long come from the lake - it's very peaceful, I was wondering what the building is in the centre of the island?" Grimes opened the little gate for Emma and talked as they left the grounds of the cottage.

"That's the bird hide Miss Maynard, Morris – I mean your uncle built it himself not long after he bought the house and grounds. All his own work"

"He did the work himself?" Emma replied surprisingly

"Yes Miss I got back from two weeks away on another estate and it was all completed and the landing stage too."

Emma tried to stifle a chuckle thinking about how things had gone from being asked what she thought she was doing to now being called Miss Maynard.

"Do you swim in the lake in summer at all?"

"Oh, good grief no miss, it's not a natural lake, it's very deep and cold on account of it being a disused flooded quarry. Water finds its own level miss, not 10 feet from the bank it drops sharply to 30 feet or more. You wait and see, in a few days' time, if this weather keeps up it will freeze over, it often does. That area is a bit of a frost pocket, I'm ashamed to say in my younger days I use to walk the ice to the island – heaven knows what I was thinking!"

"Did my uncle used to row out there and bird watch?"

"Yes miss, he loved the peace and quiet – that's why there's only one boat so he couldn't be disturbed."

Emma said goodbye to Mr Grimes and made her way back to the house, although the sun was out and the sky cloudless, she was starting to feel the cold.

Back at the house, Emma was surprised to see an old Land Rover parked near her car, the tyre marks showed it had come from the lane and up the drive. She made her way to within a few feet of the porch, when the main doors were flung open and a stern face woman in her 40's wearing a blue uniform with red piping came marching out carrying a box under her arm.

"Hello, my name is Emma Maynard, this was my uncle's house".

Emma thought for one humiliating moment the woman was going to completely ignore her and drive off but instead she put the little box on the passenger seat of the Land Rover and returned to her.

"Hello Emma, my name is Fiona I had been looking after your uncle for the last five years. I came to collect his left-over medicines and tablets - it is required they be returned and destroyed."

"I only found out yesterday what happened to him - falling down those awful steep stairs. I didn't know him but he must have been frail."

Fiona studied Emma in a cynical almost incredulous manner.

"I wouldn't say his fall was awful more likely impossible! I have to go now, even in this vehicle it will take a while to get home. Goodbye Emma, I'm sure we will meet up again."

Emma puzzled on nurse Fiona's words as the old Land Rover puffed and smoked its way past the gatehouse.

Walking back across the slushy courtyard to the utility room door Emma heard someone calling out in her direction.

"Hello, can you stop, hello!"

Emma was cold and tired and wanted a cup of tea and sit down but the bustling woman in full horse-riding apparel had other ideas.

"My name is Miss Heathcoat, I run the riding school from the stables here and I'd like a word."

Thus came the introduction from the strutting woman without pausing for breath.

"I understand you are the new owner of the estate now; well I wish to tell you right now I will not be paying full rent on the stables if the leaking roof isn't fixed and I have a valuable colt in there who needs the utmost care. Also, I found dried ragwort in the hay collected from the estate! How can I be expected to run a riding school if my horses are poisoned through negligence? I suggest you start by finding the hidden capital Morris obviously had, and spend it where it's needed!"

While this baffling diatribe was in full flow Miss Heathcoat would randomly wave a riding crop in all directions and then slap it against her jodhpurs.

"Give your mouth a rest woman, Miss Maynard has only been here less than a day, what the hell do you expect her to do about the roof on the stables right now? And if you don't like the hay from the estate go and buy your own. In future you bring your grievances to me, I'm the estate manager - you don't go bothering the owner!"

Emma looked round to see a fuming Mr Grimes standing behind her with a shotgun broken over his arm. Wounded, Miss Heathcoat flexed her riding crop and flounced off muttering into the confines of the stable block.

"Thank you Mr Grimes, I had no idea what she was going on about." Mr Grimes gave a half-smile.

"Don't mention it, Miss Maynard, the woman's world begins and ends with those bloody horses! And they have to be a collection of the foulest tempered skittish examples I've seen on any estate. Oh, and call me Bill"

"Thanks Bill I'm Emma, so you work on more than one estate - not just here?"

"Yes, Emma there's not enough land to keep me fully employed, so I split my time between here and another estate a few miles away. Many years ago these houses would have had hundreds of acres but as time passed land was sold off to farmers to help with running costs."

Emma headed back to the utility room door and while doing so she thought she may have been harsh in her first impression of Bill Grimes. She spent the afternoon idly touring the mansion. All the rooms were well furnished and decorated but somehow seemed impersonal and unwelcoming. Forgoing her own bed, she curled up on an oversized grandiose sofa in the resplendent drawing room and soon fell asleep until dinner.

The Dobbs both became avid listeners as Emma recounted to them her morning tour of the grounds and run-in with Miss Heathcoat. Frank set down his knife and fork and roared with laughter at the thought of Heathcoat being told her fortune. The conversation took on a more lugubrious air when Emma said she had briefly met nurse Fiona, although she did not mention the nurse's strange comment to them.

"She took your uncles death very hard dear; she was a

close friend to him as well as a nurse. I'm not sure if it was a sense of guilt over the fall but she's not been the same since," Pam added in a sorrowful voice.

The Dobbs stayed until just gone 9 pm before making their way to the tiny speck of light that was the gatehouse. Before leaving, Frank said he would be finished clearing the drive of snow tomorrow. No more snow was forecast but the temperatures were going to drop considerably. Emma said goodnight to them and locked the door behind them. Once again, she found herself in the prodigious mansion alone, she detested the thought of all those empty rooms, corridors and landings. After turning off the remaining lights she made her way up to her room and double-locked the door...

Emma woke at a little after 2 am, the house was even more unforgiving than the previous night. It seemed to be constantly creaking and, on more than one occasion, her imagination led her to believe footsteps were travelling the length of the landing. The only comfort she could salvage from this uncanny situation was the thought that she had locked her door - without this instilled in her mind she half expected her door to spontaneously fly open and give admittance to something unwholesome. She sat up in bed and suddenly remembered pleasant Orchard cottage and then an idea came to her. If the place was empty, and if she had to stay here much longer, why could she not move in there? It technically was her property. A shuffling from somewhere outside her door followed by a faint thud from the shadowy depths of the rambling mansion quickly made up her mind. She put her light on and spent an uneasy night wishing the minutes away until the daylight came.

Emma was up and dressed early, during the awful watches of the night she had perfected her plan for the day ahead - the many unexplained sounds served perfectly to end her vacillating. After breakfast, she would clear her car of snow and get a report on the roads, if they still seemed too bad to be travelled, she would take up residence in Orchard cottage and wait it out. However, if the going seemed good she would leave as soon as possible giving the reason as urgent business back home. Then in an uncharacteristically poltroon manner, she would hand the whole thing back to the solicitors to "dispose" of - as Osborne had called it. Fate once again intervened as it always seems to on the most carefully of laid plans. This time it was in the form of a phone call from Mr Clark from the solicitors at around 9 am just after breakfast. Emma seated herself at her uncles' desk in the princely study and raised the old fashioned faded black Bakelite phone to her ear.

"Hello this is Emma Maynard speaking"

"Hello Miss Maynard, my name is Mr Clark from Osborne, Osborne and Clark. As you know we were your late Uncles solicitors. I am aware you have already met with one of my partners regarding your inheritance. I do need to discuss a few details with you regarding various bank accounts your uncle held. My preliminary inspections have uncovered some rather unconventional transactions.

"Mr Clark I really have no idea to what you are referring can you please be more specific." There was a brief pause and papers could be heard being shuffled about rapidly.

"Oh dear this is very difficult to explain. If it wasn't for the distance, I'd have driven over but as you know we are a considerable distance away. Your uncle stayed loyal to us and never changed to a local company."

Emma was at first annoyed but then it dawned on her this phone call would be the perfect reason to excuse herself from the dreary Mansion, she politely asked Mr Clark to carry on.

"Let me explain by just focussing on your late uncles' main day to day account. The fact is there is very little money in it at present, not enough to cover the monthly outgoings and staff wages. It appears at roughly three-month intervals large sums were paid into the account that was intended to cover the usual running costs associated with a large estate." Emma cast her eyes round the room as the blether continued, there was a beautiful oil painting of the lake hanging over the fireplace. Then she asked Mr Clark how the staff were usually paid.

"Well far be it for me to judge your late uncles' idiosyncratic way of running things there but they were all paid monthly in cash - not the best of business practices. The point I'm trying to impress upon you is that your late uncle obviously had an undeclared source of revenue that we simply cannot trace. For example, some three years ago a large portion of the roof needed extensive work. I have found the receipt for the works carried out; the final bill came to £29,500. At the time the account in question was in the black to the sum of eight thousand pounds. Five days later £40,000 was paid in and the bill settled in full. It's the same over and over again Miss Maynard – money is paid in when needed which does not come from any means we can trace to your uncles' estate or other accounts."

"So, what you're trying to tell me is my uncle was bankrupt but at the same time he wasn't? Emma swivelled on the creaking chair wanting to bring the phone call to an end.

"The estate is easily worth in the region of three and a half million, all of which was your uncles, with nothing owing. I'm simply trying to inform you a cash flow problem seems to be imminent."

Emma thanked Mr Clark for his help and said she would look into it and then silently left the study.

Emma clawed at the frozen snow on the windscreen of her car, the task was further impeded by the clumsy mittens she had borrowed. She cursed herself for not clearing it all off yesterday before the frost had worked its magic on it. Pam was upstairs hoovering and as yet knew nothing of her plans to leave. She would sort the car out first then pack her holdall and announce a recall to her solicitors.

"Hello Emma do you need help with that?" Came Bill's voice from in the direction of the stables, she had been so engrossed in frantic efforts to escape she hadn't noticed him.

"Hi Bill it's frozen on hard do you have a scraper or something I could borrow please?"

"Of course, come round to the garage I'll have a rummage - Morris loved his cars he had no end of paraphernalia to keep them tip-top."

On the left-hand wall next to one of the large Range Rovers there were three lengths of metal shelving neatly crammed with waxes, sprays, lint rags, pots of paint matching the four vehicles and several chamois leathers.

"Here we are Emma, scrapers and de-icer that should do the trick but I should run the engine and put the heat on the screen too." Emma thanked Bill but instead of leaving the garage she propped herself against the shiny wing of the Range Rover.

"Bill, did you ever hear any rumours of money my uncle had hidden away or other valuables? It's important I find them if they exist at all." Bill looked disenchanted and adjusted his cap before speaking.

"I don't mean to be rude Emma, but is all this not enough? Trust me I know the value of these estates; I've put enough sweat into them over the years. I better be going now, I've things to do."

"No wait Bill you don't understand, the solicitor phoned this morning, there aren't enough funds in the bank to run the estate much longer. This sounds ungrateful but I've been dumped in this situation I want to go home and I'm tired. I also have a conscience and don't want people including yourself to be left without their wages, so do you know anything or not?" Emma banged her hand down on the roof of the Range Rover at the end of the sentence and stared directly into his eyes. Bill walked back into the garage looking both sanguine and dumbfounded.

"I can tell you something Emma, I can guarantee only the source of the story, not the validity. My oldest brother spent his life in the merchant navy and vaguely knew Morris many years ago, he told me this story when I was a young man and first came to work here. Your uncle was part of a salvage recovery team who had permission to recover precious metals and other items from sunken World War Two wrecks."

Emma was at last finding out more about her uncle and perched herself on the bonnet of the big vehicle, now an ardent listener.

"I really don't know how the whole thing works but I know anything found has to be declared, it may have to do with the nationality of the ship or the waters it sank in - but it all has to be done with the correct consent. Your uncles' team had recovered modest finds from two wrecks and were debating whether to carry on when they decided to play a hunch and discovered a sunken freighter loaded with gold and silver bars. I forget the name of the ship".

"Was it the Commissioner-General Bill?"

Bill looked slightly astonished and drew closer.

"That's it! But how did you know?" Emma quickly explained about the model in the study and asked Bill to carry on.

"I didn't often go in the study and if I did, I never really took notice of anything. Anyway, so the story goes they recovered the gold and silver but at that point, greed got the better of them and they decided to only declare a small portion of the haul. The Commissioner-General was already an old ship at the time of its sinking so they decided to collapse the cargo holds with small demolition charges after they had recovered the precious metal and declare it was impossible to salvage anymore due to the wrecks precarious condition. That is pretty much all I know; I presume they handed over a small amount of gold and silver and concealed the bulk of it away somewhere to be divided up. It wasn't a big team so we can only wonder how much they got away with – that is if any of this actually happened."

Emma slid off the bonnet and thought things over for a while, it would explain how her uncle could have afforded the estate and the mysterious timely cash injections.

"Who did the gold belong to Bill? Did no-one recheck the wreck again?"

The two walked back out and headed to the front of the house.

"Could be foreign currency or gold reserves a country didn't want to fall into the hands of the Nazis or could just have been smuggled. During the sea war, the Germans were conducting unrestricted submarine warfare which meant they would sink any freighter or tanker of a country they were at war with without warning. They had no real interest in the cargo they were just told to sink ships. I've no idea if anyone checked on the wreck again. I would imagine they covered their tracks and as I said the ship was already very old when it went down, so collapsed cargo holds would have been more than believable."

The two had reached the snowbound car by now and Bill said he had to leave to attend to duties on the other estate. Before he left, Emma asked him if he really believed the story about the gold. He gave a snort and said he would like to but even if it were true the secret of any hidden treasure probably died with her uncle.

Emma eventually cleared her car of the snow and as an added precaution placed a flat sheet of white cardboard that she carried in her boot as a make-do frost cover across the windscreen and anchored it with the wiper blades.

Returning indoors she was relieved to hear Pam still upstairs so she quietly made herself a cup of tea and paced the kitchen - sometimes stopping to bang her hands in frustration on the big cooking range. Her mind was racing a mile a minute. Bill's story would explain everything - even the model in the study. Just then Frank came in through the utility room and said the roads were all clear now but a very heavy frost was on the cards for tonight. Emma exchanged a few pleasantries but was beginning to get the impression the honeymoon was over and before long the couple would rightly be asking her what the future held for the estate and themselves. Just then Pam appeared with her usual jovial mood and the pair announced they were going to town for some supplies in case the weather turned again. Emma declined their invitation to join them and instead said she would go for a walk later.

The Victorian walnut dressing table was quickly emptied of the few items of clothing Emma had deposited within its deep bun handled draws and then shoved firmly back in place. She caught sight of herself in the oval mirror and stopped her marked preparations. The face staring back at her was of someone about to run away. She looked a mess – her usually straight hair was kinked in places and her brown eyes looked tired. Pacing about the room she spoke out loud in an angry tone,

"Why leave me all this without even a single letter or any guidance?" She stopped at once and plunged her hand into her jeans pocket, the word letter had jogged her memory. The note! She had forgotten all about it up until now. Unfolding it carefully she read it out loud twice and then tossed it onto the little bow-fronted mahogany bedside table. It made less sense in the cold light of day than it did the first time she had inadvertently came across it.

"Hopeless!" she exclaimed and flinging herself on the freshly made bed and closing her eyes. Now she would have to wait for the Dobbs to return before she could leave. Her watering eyes opened and eventually after a marked endeavour focused on the little note again. Due to its half curled up stance on the bedside table and her recumbent position she found herself viewing it at a different angle. Only the first letter from each line was now visible. She sat up in bed and expeditiously picked up the note and folded the right half over to cover all but the first letters. When read downwards they gave the message: "*in my study lake*".

Emma felt a brief rush of excitement wake her from her apathy as she warily left her room and headed down the grand staircase. Although the mansion was once again deserted, she was careful not to make a noise on the gleaming white tiles. The study was silent with a slight scent of polish emanating from the unblemished furniture.

"Well uncle I'm in the study and I'm looking at the lake painting," she said out loud and then at once felt foolish. The oil painting was unsigned but had been executed with considerable skill. It depicted the setting in full summer, the island was bursting with green leafy trees dotted with smaller yellow and orange shrubbery. The water was a bluey turquoise and soothingly calm, every so often random patches of dark green reeds could be seen poking out of the glassy surface close to the bank. The landing stage on the island was prominent and had a white boat moored to one of its posts. The bird hide was visible nestled in the trees and looked restful underneath a brilliant sun and drifting white clouds.

There was only one thing for it Emma thought and stealthily dragged a large red leather ottoman over to the picture. She quickly stood onto it, and being extremely careful not to hit the display light above the landscape with the ornate guilt frame, she raised the large picture free of its wall mounting. She had to step down quickly before the full weight of the picture became too much. She suddenly burst out laughing at how careful she was being, it was her house and everything in it. If she wanted to examine an old painting she could. A quick look at the bare wall behind the painting immediately dispelled the rather fanciful idea of a hidden wall safe. Gently turning the large frame around, a fresh white envelope was at once visible against the dusty brown canvas back. The sticky tape that held it in place looked fresh, it was almost as if it had been placed there yesterday.

After a considerable effort, she replaced the oil painting to its rightful place and then dragged the heavy ottoman back to the other side of the fireplace from whence it came.

Leaving the study, she glanced around the reception hall and down the dim corridor leading to the main doors then scurried back up the stairs and into her room.

Emma carefully opened the white envelope and removed a single sheet of watermarked blue writing paper. Walking to the window she unfolded the paper and read every word of it in exhaustive detail.

"Dear Emma,

If you have found this note then please forgive the rather whimsical lengths to which I have gone in order to conceal it. I have recently discovered I may have good reason to be cautious.

As the new owner of Marsden Manor, you will need a ready supply of capital for the everyday running of the estate and house.

I will be sending three information packs to my solicitors which will give you full instructions and where a source of revenue can be located. This note is merely a cautionary measure I have implemented in light of recent events.

Visit the island on the lake Emma, it will offer support but please be careful and only take one step at a time.

Fondest regards

Morris

A wave of emotions flowed through Emma's mind, at first, she was exhilarated at the contents of the letter but this was soon replaced with a more sinister disquieting feeling. The letter mentioned being cautious as if he feared something in his own house, and the other note asked her to be wary of others. A wave of trepidation hit her - had she said too much to Bill about the financial situation here? He seemed nice but she didn't know him or anyone here anymore than they knew her… Then there was the comment nurse Fiona made about her uncle's fall being impossible…

Maybe it was being in arrears of two decent night's sleep combined with the general upheaval mixed with the whole far-fetched peculiar situation that served to trick her mind - but she sensed there was something sinister and duplicitous at work that watched over her with a wicked interest.

Taking advantage of the empty kitchen Emma made herself a bite to eat, and while in the process of hurriedly eating, formulated a quick plan. She would visit the island today, getting there wouldn't be a problem providing the boat was in good order. The only place anything could be securely concealed must be the little bird hide. Maybe a secret floor or something built into the walls. She felt sure if she could get into the hide there would be another hidden note or something leading her to… she was going to use the word "treasure" but that seemed ludicrous. Supposing the gold story was true, it didn't necessarily mean that there was gold hidden over there now. Her uncle could well have converted it into hard currency in the elapsed time - but that would mean careful storage so as not to degrade. She stopped and glanced over at all the utensils hanging in their respected higgledy-piggledy places.

"Tools or gardening implements, I must find something to take with me," she murmured, while threading her arms into the big coat and slipping on the wellington boots.

The air was bitter as she crossed the courtyard and stable block, Miss Heathcoat exited from the furthest stall wheeling a barrow. She managed to elicit a brief hello and then disappeared behind the building. Emma carried on walking until she reached the garage, and then ducked out of sight. The stables had a good-sized concrete building joined to them before the first stall. That had to be a tool shed of some kind - if only she would stop strutting about and clear off, Emma thought. Heathcoat came and went from one side of the stables to the other, hay was distributed tack was cleaned down and put away before finally she closed all the doors and departed on a very unwieldy quad bike.

Rushing over to the shed Emma quickly tried the lock with a likely key she had selected from her bunch while waiting for Heathcoat to exit the scene. It simply read *"storage 1"* thankfully the lock turned and she entered quickly closing the door behind her. Two ride-on mowers were parked end to end in the centre of the room, the first one facing a padlocked roller shutter at the rear of the building. All round the walls hung a profusion of tools some she recognised such as spades, forks and hoes while others were alien to her. On a large metal topped workbench there were chainsaws, hedge trimmers and other power tools. Emma felt almost like a burglar as she grabbed a hessian sack that was covering the seat of the nearest mower and started searching through a tool chest tucked underneath the bench.

Selecting a hacksaw, crowbar, trowel and screwdriver her attention then turned to the undergrowth on the island, she would need something that could clear a path to the bird hide. Glancing over to the wall she glimpsed a vicious looking machete and decided it would do admirably as it wasn't too bulky. She adroitly loaded her acquired tools into the dusty hessian sack and left the storage shed making sure to lock the door behind her.

Emma zipped her coat up against the plummeting temperature and headed towards the little hidden boathouse. She was going out to that island to seek the solution to this situation and was determined not to leave until the answer was found.

Knowing exactly where she was going this time Emma had taken a much more direct diagonal route across the sprawling ice-capped fields and now found herself staring out at the unforgiving dark blue depths and esoteric unspoilt island. Icicles hung in gaggles from the untidy little thatched roof of the boathouse. After a quick glance around, Emma stooped and entered the boathouse - gently placing the assorted tools down in the bottom of the boat. She then collected the two grimy oars from the corner and climbed into the rowing boat with her back to the bow. Although the craft looked watertight, she examined the inside bottom as a precaution before going any further – it appeared fine with no apparent leaks. The island couldn't have been more than seventy feet away but remembering Bills caution on how quickly the lake increased in depth, she had no intention of getting halfway out only to discover the boat was holed. Next, she untied the rope from the rusty iron post and took a deep breath before firmly shoving off from the post using one of the oars.

The momentum from the shove had the desired effect and she was soon clear of the boathouse and mooring. Next she loaded the two oars into their respected rowlocks and placed them into the water. It was almost a dead straight course over to the landing stage on the island but Emma being out of practice had soon veered off slightly. She had tried to let the oars run through the water as cleanly as possible but parts of the lake were covered in sheets of ice that hadn't been visible from the shore and had thrown off her stroke. Eventually using the right oar only, she managed to correct the course and moved the boat back to the left. As she was engaged in this ungainly procedure, she became acutely aware of how visible the white boat must be on the still blue lake - maybe Bill or the Dobbs were watching her at this very moment.

Eventually after what seemed an age and a few more navigational corrections the white bows of the boat collided with a set of rusty steps in an uncoordinated manner. Emma adroitly stood up in the boat and securely fastened the rope to one of the posts and then collected the sack of tools. The landing stage had evidently been built to easily accommodate another two boats the size of hers. There were two sets of chunky corroded metal steps leading into the water on each of the longest sides as well as the set she had collided with, that faced the mainland. The wooden planks looked rotten in places with the snow and ice making them treacherous. Gently climbing up Emma paused for a moment and then proceeded along the mouldy looking wood timber. The whole thing seemed in desperate need of repair, and glancing over at the sets of rusty metal steps revealed many of them to be missing. Safely off of the landing stage Emma glanced back at the vast white field and little boathouse. Nothing moved in the wispy frigid air - no curious spectators on the bank watching in perplexity - just a cold loneliness.

Turning to the island she was surprised how big the baron leafless trees were compared to viewing them from the shore. The bird hide was not far away. The machete came into its own at clearing the way. Dead willow and birch branches were strewn around and intertwined in dense protective tangles; thorn bushes scraped at her coat as she drew closer to the peculiar little structure. The unspoilt snow hid all manner of trip hazards including tree stumps and dips. After a few clumsy stumbles which nearly served to make her a victim of the lethal machete, Emma arrived at the narrow little door and examined it carefully. It was no more than three feet wide and bellied out at the top and bottom as a testament to the harsh weather and neglect which it had endured. A rusty hasp and staple halfway down the narrow portal was secured only with a skilfully carved wooden peg. Emma was bemused but also relieved at this, the time saving levering an obstinate padlock off the door with the crowbar would be well spent inside instead. She placed the machete down out of harm's way. The narrow observation windows were boarded up from the inside, so the first job would be to take these down so a proper search could be undertaken in the light. Pushing the door open slowly Emma stepped cautiously inside.

The soggy mouldering boards obligingly left their resting place and the dark damp confines of the dilapidated hide once again saw the light of day. The light also brought with it a slight disappointment, because looking round in the bitter air, and under its clarity, revealed there was very little contained within the rotting structure.

Directly underneath the observation windows was a dusty old bench bereft of anything of interest, partly tucked underneath this was a padded high-backed stool now covered in a nasty looking white mould. In the right-hand corner, a rusty potbellied stove was still waiting impatiently to be brought to life again. Above this at shoulder height was a short length of shelving which had a few jars and a rusty biscuit tin resting on it. Emma divested herself of her gloves briefly and set about examining the objects. The jars - all three of them contained nails and screws. So it was with a growing trepidation that Emma gently took the old tin box down from its resting place and laid it on the bench…

Nothing! A medium-sized hammer and two screwdrivers! The all to identifiable feeling of disappointment which had washed over her many times since this bizarre adventure began, once again took hold of her.

"I've just about had enough of this bloody nonsense uncle! Why can't you have used a bank like everybody else?!" Emma shouted out loud in a scolding tone while glancing around yet again.

There was a little card table in the left-hand corner and above that stapled to the walls were tattered posters and charts all pertaining to bird watching. Emma studied each one carefully but they had not been doctored or contained any hidden meanings. Getting more frustrated and desperate, Emma examined the ageing wooden boards that made up the floor and even tried the cold steel of the crowbar on likely looking loose sections - but nothing gave way and no cunningly hidden trap doors made themselves known. The smell of decay from the hide and anti-climax of the expedition made Emma call an end to the search and step outside. She hadn't noticed on entering the hide but on the inside of the door were some safety instructions on climbing in and out of a moored boat, these were typed in large letters. Emma looked them over but they seemed harmless and almost child-like in their simplicity. Feeling beaten Emma re-boarded the windows, collected her tools and headed for the landing stage and her waiting boat.

Emma placed the sack of tools down in the bottom of the boat and stared at the rapidly freezing water as it idly lapped up against the chunky steps. Something was nagging at her… something about those instructions on the door of the hide seemed familiar to her but she knew not how. She carried on staring at the steps leading down into the dark depths. Carefully crossing the icy landing-stage again, she returned to the hide and flung open the door, she then withdrew the note from her uncle instructing her to visit the island.

"I knew something rang a bell!" she exclaimed. It was the instruction which read "For maximum caution and safety only take one step at a time". Her uncle had implored she only take one step at a time in his concealed note… Emma cautiously smiled and said,

"I think I know why you built such a large landing stage uncle" and returned to her boat.

A long judicious gouge curtesy of the crowbar at last rewarded the weary searcher… beneath the tarnished surface of those now all too ingot resembling steps that flanked each side of the landing stage, gold glistened… Emma selected the hacksaw and set to work. The search was over and the next stage of this troubled adventure had begun… Who to trust?

Later that afternoon Emma informed Pam she was going to make some calls in town and be back the following day weather permitting. Pam looked her over rather cautiously as if expecting an explanation for her departure.

"It's nothing to worry about Pam, I just need to sort a few bits and pieces." This rather bland statement was greeted with the reaction it deserved and Pam looked a bit upset. Emma, not wanting to reveal anything yet then quickly spoke again to quell any tension.

"I know you and Frank must be wondering what will happen to the estate now that my uncle has gone... That is why I need to leave for a day or two, I have some items to look into with my solicitor but I think everything will be fine." This second declaration seemed to serve its purpose and that friendly smile returned to Pam's face and she spoke.

"Don't you go driving on these roads in that car of yours dear, you take one of the Range Rovers. They are insured for anyone to use and are only parked there doing nothing, you will be safer dear." Emma offered a dozen reason why she would rather take her own car but each was politely dismissed.

Within 30 minutes Bill had been drafted in to give her a brief tutorial on the controls of the massive Range Rover, after confusing her totally with the functions of various bits of equipment he must have sensed her unease and then jokingly said,

"Or you could do what I do... just put it in drive and floor it!"

Emma laughed, "I think I can handle that alright."

Bill looked round and then asked her if she had found out any more about the financial problem which they had spoken. Emma said not and thanked him for his help and then frugally pulled away in the impressive machine. She hated telling lies but something wasn't quite what it appeared to be somehow. Reaching the gates, she stopped and had a quick recap on the events so far. The only slip up she had made regarding the exploration of the island was to leave the damn machete over there but that surely would not be missed? Other than that, she was quite sure her presence on the island had gone unnoticed. She had even gone as far as declining Frank's offer to carry her bag to the car - he might wonder at the newly acquired weight of it now it had the dirty old ingot contained therein! She needed a night away from that restless old mansion with its watchful oppressiveness. Tomorrow she would have the ingot tested as a formality, but first, she had a call to make in town and an explanation to be given. Emma slipped the silently idling black machine into drive and pulled away from her estate and along the frozen road.

It wasn't hard tracking down nurse Fiona in such a small town. Emma had called at the local Doctors surgery and introduced herself and was informed that if she walked over to the pharmacy, Fiona would be calling in there as per her routine that afternoon. It was dusk already and a frost had already started to descend as Emma paced about outside the tiny façade of the pharmacy. The familiar sound of the geriatric Land Rover met her cold ears, it lumbered into view and parked a little way down the street. Fiona got out wearing a heavy coat and woollen hat pulled well down….well Emma presumed it was her in the dusk light.

"Excuse me, Fiona?" Emma called out while approaching the muffled-up figure. Maybe it wasn't her after all as the figure didn't react to her calling out. Emma repeated her words.

"Who is that? Oh, hello Emma, sorry I have to wear ear defenders as this old crate is so loud and also heaters were not invented when it was made."

Emma laughed and then replied, "Well, you said we would meet again so I wonder if I could have five minutes of your time? I have a car over there and it has a fancy heater too." Fiona collected her prescriptions first then the two of them made their way over to the Range Rover.

"I have driven this a few times too, it's nice isn't it?" Fiona remarked.

Emma nodded and agreed it was growing on her. Then came an awkward silence until Emma in a much more direct manner than she had rehearsed on her way to town, asked her what she meant by her uncles' death due to a fall being impossible. There was a long pause before Fiona spoke.

"Just what I said, it was impossible. I can see your stay at the estate has given you a dose of its uneasy quality, you look tired Emma." Before Emma could reply Fiona carried on.

"Did you ever have to fast because you were having blood tests done the next day? Morris had to a few times a year. Usually, he would have lunch then nothing until the tests at around ten the following morning." Emma looked confused.

"The night before your uncle died, he was fasting; he

had a light lunch and was not allowed to eat or drink anything until the blood tests were taken. I left him in bed at 10 pm I said I would call at 9 am to run him to the hospital - in this very car! Why do you suppose he would then decide to get up in the middle of the night and go downstairs to make himself a cup of tea - that was the prevailing theory was it not? Sorry I should have said - why do you suppose he would go down to the kitchen using the servant's stairs (which he hated and never used once in all the time I had known him) intending to make a cup of tea with sugar which he knew would invalidate his results?"

Emma had asked for an explanation and she had been delivered one in a frosty tone to match the weather.

"Don't take this the wrong way Fiona, I know you were fond of my uncle but isn't it possible that due to his age and needing a nurse…"

Fiona sharply interrupted, "I will save you the fumbling Emma - your uncle did not have any form of dementia! He did the times crossword daily and was still fluent in three languages. His limbs and organs were failing Emma not his mind."

Emma thanked Fiona for her help and apologised if she had caused any offence. Fiona replied that none was taken and it was a pity that despite her protestations at the time to the coroner's verdict no further action was taken.

As Fiona was leaving the vehicle, Emma without really knowing why, said "Can I trust you if I need you up at the estate?"

Fiona nodded and softly said, "Your uncle trusted me with his life and someone or something took it while I wasn't there to protect him. All I can do now is find out what happened. I'm not jumping to conclusions Emma, but he would never have used those stairs - they frightened him because they are so steep, he made me swear never to let on to anyone about that, I think it was out of pride. Go back to your uncles' room Emma and you too will understand my suspicions. Take care and be safe."

Fiona then crammed a small white scrap of paper into Emma's hand and departed.

After the brief meeting Emma visited the local pub for a hurried meal and then got back in her newly acquired car and drove - and continued driving until her body had told her to stop, by which time she was just over halfway back to her flat. While she drove, she mulled over the situation while the Range Rover effortlessly motored on through the freezing darkness. She had solved the riddle but was no further forward and the meeting with Fiona had served only to make her more perturbed. She simply couldn't believe any of the people she had met would harm her uncle - they had been employed and trusted for years. Then she thought about her cargo...the gold ingot. Maybe that was the cause of her uncle's apparent "accident", - had a long-forgotten accomplice returned to settle an old score over it? Or maybe the person her uncle used to convert the gold into currency had felt cheated?

Emma could drive no further, she pulled in at a large pub which thankfully had a vacant room and dragged herself up the stairs to bed. Before she fell into a feverish sleep, she sarcastically thought to herself that just a few days ago she was wrestling with a completely different set of problems to the ones she faced now. A letter from a solicitor had literally deposited her into the middle of an Alistair Maclean novel…and she was scared.

Emma returned to Marsden Manor two days later and by a complete coincidence found herself pulled up in the exact same spot as she had been on her first nervous visit and feeling much the same if not worse - she was now laden with secrets and a feeling of dread. She stared at the tall entrance pillars some 50 feet away, every intuition told her to turn around and place everything in the hands of the solicitors. It had snowed more in her absentia and what ground was to be seen looked frozen solid. She drove forward and crossed the threshold of her estate once more.

This time Frank had met her at the gatehouse and after a few pleasantries she continued on to the esoteric mansion. It didn't look any more welcoming than the first time it had presented itself - nor would it ever. Frank had informed her that Pam was cleaning in the holiday cottage.

Emma unlocked the front door after finally selecting the right key and made her way upstairs and back to her allotted room. The unwelcoming aura exuded on the exterior was replicated inside but seemed multiplied, the house was particularly gloomy and sombre.

After a half-hearted unpack, she made her way down to the kitchen and while the kettle took an age to boil, went over things in her mind. The gold was indeed genuine, after dissecting a good size chunk in the safety of her flat she paid a visit to a jeweller she knew fairly well in town. Its unit of purity was proven to be 18 karat - which he explained meant it had been melted down from pure gold of 24 karat and then copper and silver added, this was done because pure gold is too soft to make jewellery from. He paid handsomely for the chunk of precious metal and seemed more than happy with her explanation of finding it on a beach in Cornwall while on holiday. She left with a roll of crisp notes and the knowledge she had rather amateurishly just fenced stolen goods!

She would give herself two days snooping and if nothing else came to light, would inform the correct people. A good search of the study was undoubtedly called for - there must be contacts or more information her uncle meant to send to her. In the meantime, she would act dumb and play everything down - the thought that her uncle may well have been murdered was still terrifying.

As a last-ditch protective measure, Emma had taken an added precaution almost like an insurance policy while she was back home. It was very simple but the sobering fact was if she had to call upon it, then it would be to save her life…

Pam visited later that day and soon busied herself bustling around the grand old rooms clad in her floral apron. Much later Emma and the Dobbs were having a drink in the kitchen when a knock came on the back door and Bill appeared,

"Mind if I come in folks?" Bill was cordially greeted

and another cup of tea squeezed out of the brown teapot. Emma seized on the opportunity and quickly spoke before the conversation turned to more trivial matters,

"Actually, I'm glad you are all here I need to tell you something. Bill is that Heathbrick woman out there?"

Bill laughed, "It's Heathcoat Emma and no she is off risking her life on one of her charming horses, probably pulling herself out of a ditch right now."

"Ok well perhaps you could relay this to her then please? I have been to see the solicitors and everything is in hand and there is no danger of anything drastic happening to the estate. Things are taking longer because there are a lot of loose ends to tie up. It's compounded by the fact I know very little of legal matters and they have to explain it in triplicate most of the time."

Frank Dobbs spoke first, "Thank you for the update Emma, I would be lying if I said we had not been worried."

Bill gave Emma a half-smile and a nod which she reciprocated and then announced she was going for a walk to clear a headache brought on by the drive up.

There was little more than an hour of light left as Emma set out - she passed her forlorn car which hadn't moved since she arrived - it seemed like weeks ago. The make-do cardboard she had placed on the windscreen had merged with the rest of the car owing to an inch or more of frozen snow. She knew where she was heading and in 10 minutes was once again staring out at the little island - the keeper of the *Commissioner-Generals* sunken cargo.

As Bill had predicted the artificial lake had frozen over giving the impression the island was floating on a cloud. She tested the ice with her foot, it seemed solid and no cracking could be heard, then remembering how deep the water was, she withdrew her foot and backed away. She was also relieved to see no footprints other than hers were apparent and the boat was just how she had left it in the little squat boathouse, meaning no one had visited this place during her time away. She trudged back to the house, deciding her next move.

Emma stared across the tundra at the little gatehouse, it was nearly 11pm and still a solitary light burned. She had turned down Pam's offer of cooking her a meal and instead said she would get an early night. One of the front-facing bedrooms on the right of the mansion afforded the best view of the gatehouse but waiting in its cold vastness was beginning to pray on her nerves- especially as she was in the dark! Finally, the light went out and by the illumination of her phone torch, she headed down the corridor and descended the cold stairs. The house seemed particularly noisy that night, random creaks and groans came and went as if testing her nerves to breaking point and a cold wind brushed her face. Once inside the study, the search was on! Although the windows were rear-facing, she drew the thick velvet curtains as an added precaution and only then turned on the main ceiling lights as well as the brass desk lamp.

For nearly two hours every scrap of paperwork was examined, every drawer, cupboard and shelf went over but none yielded anything more productive than farm supply receipts and laborious minutes from round table meetings.

Emma precisely replaced everything and then stole herself for the next task... one she had been putting off. She needed to search her uncle's bedroom...

The dour atmosphere of the house was increasing as Emma turned the handle and entered her late uncles' room... the windows faced the front-drive so this search would be undertaken by torchlight. She didn't suspect the Dobbs of any wrongdoing but still thought it wiser not to let them see a light on in a room she had no real business in. Her thoughts kept coming back to Bill...he had the knowledge of the sunken gold, had he whetted her appetite to find it for him? And was he now waiting for her to report back? She looked at the walnut writing bureau and started to search in earnest. Some of the smaller drawers had to be unlocked with keys from her bunch but again nothing was forthcoming. The bureau seemed remarkably clean and free of even a note pad...perhaps too clean. It was now well past one in the morning and Emma was exhausted. The darkroom was eerie in the torchlight, under its restricted beams, the small army of armchairs seemed to be on manoeuvres around the room. Before she left to give in to the call to sleep, Emma made her way over to the two doors and shakily opened them... The door on the left revealed a good size wet room all gleaming - more of Pam's handy work. The other door gave entrance to a large walk-in wardrobe containing crisp rows of her Uncles clothes silently hanging. She was on the point of leaving when she noticed there was an alcove in the left corner of the wardrobe, almost certainly deliberately hidden by a large shoe-rack... Emma advanced and shone the torch into the darkness of the recess.

"Went downstairs to get a cup of tea my ass," Emma muttered as she cast her eye over a small tiled kitchen with two units, stainless steel kettle and a tabletop fridge. Even if Fiona had made up the blood test story (which she didn't think she had) this certainly blew the prevailing theory out of the water. Emma returned to her own room and soon fell asleep, although she had no way of knowing it then, it would be the last time she would ever sleep in the disastrous old mansion again...

Waking a little after 10 Emma washed and dressed and hurried downstairs to the deserted kitchen, a handwritten note from Pam informed her bacon and eggs were in the fridge. After indulging in a full cooked breakfast with all the trimmings, Emma was about to commence a daylight search of the study when Bill appeared at the back door,

"Hope you don't mind me calling Emma, I didn't get the chance to talk to you yesterday. Have you found out anything about the gold? I'm only asking because of what you said about the approaching financial situation here." Emma noticed he had a disquietude in his eyes which unsettled her.

"Sorry Bill I wish I had, the solicitors are looking into my uncle's accounts and seem to think their first appraisal of the situation was a bit hasty. I will hear more soon, you know what they are like - everything has to be done at their pace."

"I understand, but you will let me know? And if I were you, I wouldn't tell anyone." Emma felt alarm bells ringing but downplayed it beautifully.

"I expect it was all a yarn Bill, catch you later."

Emma went upstairs to put on her heavy jumper, she was toying with the idea of looking over all the rooms but that seemed ridiculous. She entered the silence of her uncles' chamber again and walked to the window, her thoughts ran in an unwholesome manner as she pondered the latest developments. Why did Pam go along with the theory her uncle went downstairs in the middle of the night to make a cup of tea when she knew there was a kitchen in his room? Who had gone to the length of trying to conceal the kitchen? Emma screwed her face up, she couldn't do this anymore it was like a horrid murder mystery; she had even questioned why Fiona made the journey to collect unused medication, was there something wrong with it?

"Oh shut up Emma it was Fiona who alerted you!" she screamed at herself in disgust. A far-off movement caught her eye, the Dobbs were walking up from the gatehouse towards the mansion carrying shopping bags. Emma raised her eyes to heaven and couldn't help wondering if they hung around the house as much as this when her uncle was alive and then she recoiled to her room - she really was not in the mood to speak to them. The time dragged pitifully until dinner - Pam could not be put off a second night in making a fine meal and the three of them chatted informally while outside a freezing fog enveloped the estate and increased the isolation.

After dinner, Frank excused himself and said he needed to bleed the upstairs radiators as the house seemed colder than usual. Pam wouldn't hear of Emma helping with the washing up so she awkwardly perched herself against the stove in silence. Not long after the commencement of the washing up Emma noticed Pam's shoulders sag and her head bow down towards the sink - then came a sobbing.

"Pam, Pam, whatever is the matter? The washing up can't be that bad" she joked trying to ease the situation and cover her own embarrassment. Pam's solid frame quivered slightly and she regained her composure.

"I'm sorry Emma, really I am. You have enough to deal with without me going to pieces on you."

"Don't be silly tell me what's up," Emma motioned Pam to sit down.

"It's Frank's younger brother, he's been desperately ill for months now, he needs all kinds of treatments if he's to last the year out."

"I am sorry Pam I had no idea, what on earth is wrong with him?"

Pam stared at the kitchen table and seemed to be making a concentrated effort to fend off more tears.

"Some sort of blood cancer or something, we have already used the money your uncle kindly left us to pay for private treatments. He is the only family Frank has."

Emma felt sick, here she was, the accidental millionaire who had inherited a fortune and found another but it had made little impression on her - as if she were an ungrateful child.

"I need to make a phone call Pam, make us both a cup of tea please. I can help you with this I promise, it's the least I can do."

Emma produced Fiona's phone number from her jeans pocket and picked up the antique telephone in the study – it was useless trying to use her mobile.

"Hello, Fiona its Emma. I had to tell someone I can't go on keeping things to myself anymore. I should have told you before."

"Tell me what Emma? Are you ok?"

"My uncle did have a secret hoard hidden on the estate, I have found it and I'm going to put it to good use. I think it may have been the cause of his death too."

"Emma listen to me, don't do anything rash please we need to…."

"Fiona? Fiona are you there?"

Emma repeated this again but the phone was dead. She replaced the receiver and re-joined Pam in the kitchen.

"Sorry to leave you Pam, the phone isn't working it went dead."

Pam was drooped over the kitchen sink with her back to Emma, she spoke without turning around, "It often goes dead dear; I don't think that old phone helps matters much."

Emma walked over to Pam and put a hand on her

shoulder. "Don't worry Pam when Frank comes down, I will explain things."

Emma turned towards the kettle but at that point she felt a tremendous blow connect with the back of her head and she tumbled forward to the kitchen floor!

"Come down Frank! You were right! The sob story worked like a charm - she had found out!"

Emma regained her senses and sat up against the stout leg of the table. Pam leaned over her with a satisfying grin playing about her podgy lips. Just then heavy footsteps approached the kitchen and Frank Dobbs hastily entered carrying a shotgun in his left hand. Emma felt sick... she had played right into the hands of her uncles' murderers - and now she was powerless. Frank joined his wife's side and they both looked down on her as if studying a stricken animal in some awful trap. Emma knew these two were playing for keeps and her life now hung by a thread.

"What did she say love?" inquired Frank Dobbs without taking his eyes off Emma and keeping the barrels of the shotgun levelled down at her.

"Well, she phoned that nosey nurse and told her she'd found Morris's hidden money."

Frank snorted at hearing this and gloatingly informed Emma there was a hidden extension and phone on the wall near the fireplace which was conveniently covered over with a large copper frying pan.

Emma was seething and retorted, "I've never spoken to

murderers before. So - which one of you took his life?"

Pam replied immediately in an indignant tone, "He brought it on himself, it was an accident. When Frank found out first hand from Morris what he was planning to do, he became so angry he gave him such a clump it killed him on the spot."

"That's enough Pam, what else did she say on the phone?"

Pam informed him that she had cut the connection before she had a chance to tell the nurse anything.

"That's good love, she has caused enough trouble at the inquest with her theories, so where is it all hidden? She told you before you thumped her, I take it?"

Pam sheepishly reported back that she had got carried away in the heat of the moment and hadn't been thinking. Frank Dobbs turned scarlet then erupted.

"You bloody stupid woman! How could you forget the most important thing? Now we are almost back where we started!"

Pam retorted back that he had started the whole thing by killing Morris in the first place. This seemed to bring on a stalemate and after a few seconds silence, Frank composed himself and was once again malign and cunning.

"Go down to the gates and close them Pam. If this bitch has phoned that nurse, I don't want her driving up here shoving her nose in again."

Pam quickly nodded almost as if happy to be trusted with a task again and then put on her coat and left via the back door.

"Get up and sit on the chair," came the cold instruction.

Emma did as she was told. Frank was playing it carefully and made sure he remained a good five feet away at all times to prevent her from making a lunge for the gun. She knew she had about 10, maybe 15 minutes at the most to somehow overpower Frank before Pam came back from the main gate, if not they could keep her pinned down indefinitely. First, she wanted answers.

"Why did you do it Frank after all these years? Had enough of being in the gatehouse and wanted to move into the mansion?"

He shook his head and laughed. "You've no idea at all, I couldn't give a damn about the estate! I've lived here long enough already. We've run around after him for years, looked after him you name it! We both knew he had no family so just assumed that when he passed away, we would get the estate, or at least a good pay-off."

Emma listened in a sickening fascination as Dobbs explained how he became a murderer.

"It was fairly common knowledge Morris had hidden a large amount somewhere here, that idiot thought he was so clever but it was obvious. Wages paid in cash and unexplained large sums of money paid in quarterly. I had looked at the books from time to time. Things seemed to be going in our favour then the daft old fool, like so many before him, started getting sentimental in his old age and your name kept being mentioned."

Emma remained silent and fixed her eyes on the fat brown teapot with its scalding cargo that sat in the centre of the kitchen table.

"We tried to monitor his phone line via the extension but he nearly always made sure he was alone in the house before he made business calls. We had our worst fears confirmed when Pam came across a bill from a private investigator that he had engaged to trace you! I knew it, I just knew you would cop the lot! But I had to be sure, so I decided to search his bureau one night".

Emma tried to hold back the tears as the sordid confession kept coming. Almost without knowing she had stealthily turned the teapot round so the handle faced her. She had to distract Frank somehow.

"I didn't have to search very hard to find what I was looking for; it was evident from a letter he was drafting that he had already made the most significant adjustments to his will and lodged them with his solicitor. The letter wasn't finished but he actually referred to you as his heir! My blood began to boil, I knew I had to control myself and let the old fool finish the letter the next day so I could learn more. I was on the point of leaving when without my knowing he had risen from his bed and caught me red-handed."

"So, you murdered him on the spot as your wife put it."

Frank shook the gun at Emma and seemed at the point

of exploding.

"Shut up you bitch! I gave him a chance! I demanded he explain everything and change his will to favour me. He then informed me I was sacked; can you believe the old git? He thought I was going to calmly accept it and walk out and pack my bags. Such a temper came over me I lashed out and hit him - sent him clean across the room. It was an accident, and I sure as hell won't be going to prison for it."

"So, you put his dressing gown and slippers on him and flung him down the servant stairs Frank? Then cleaned any traces of his appalling murder from his bedroom and then returned to your cosy gatehouse, is that the rest?"

Before Dobbs could even offer any sort of tawdry reply Emma cut in again.

"But you slipped up Frank, in fact, more than once - my uncle never used those stairs they disagreed with him. Oh, and the feeble notion of him going downstairs for a cup of tea – while ignoring the perfectly equipped kitchen virtually in his room, which one of you two had tried to hide - is a dead duck too. He was fasting that night for blood tests in the morning. I guess you need more practice at snooping and murdering Frank."

Dobbs outburst almost cost Emma her life, he crashed his hand down on the worktop and then took aim...

"Just one more comment and I swear I'll fire this at you point-blank - Morris got what he deserved and you will the same!"

Eight minutes had elapsed since Pam had left the kitchen - she would be on the return journey now; time was running out.

"You can imagine how disappointed we were after your uncle's accident. We knew you would be coming to claim the estate but we had no idea what information the old fool had sent you or what type of person you were. After our first chat in the kitchen it soon dawned on Pam and I that you were a sad loner - the sort of person who goes missing without drawing much interest. I also took the liberty of looking through your tatty bag while you were out playing lady of the manor the first morning - the scant information you had received partially confirmed that you knew less than us about any hidden wealth. So, all we could do was sit and wait to see if that was indeed the case or if you would lead us to the doddering old fools fabled hidden fortune - which you did."

It was now 10 minutes since Pam had gone, Emma knew she had to draw some reaction from Dobbs to get him to lower the gun long enough to launch her attack!

"If I go missing or have one of your made to measure accidents it will be as good as handing yourself in to the police station, is that what you want?"

Dobbs stayed silent, as Emma continued.

"I have written down all my evidence and that of Fiona and left it to be opened with my uncles' solicitors in the event of my disappearance or death. I explained I feared my life was in danger. Do you think the police will buy a second tragedy?"

Emma could see Frank turning white as he wrestled with this dilemma but the elevation of the barrels remained fixed on her.

"You're bluffing - and even if you are not, I will take my chances, it's gone too far to stop now. If the police come calling, I have something in mind that will satisfy their plodding minds. So, if you are all done then I think it's more than time you satisfied my curiosity and told me where the hoard is, and what it is!"

"It's a standoff Frank if I don't tell you there is nothing you can do, it's my best chance of staying alive. As soon as I tell you... I'll have an accident."

Frank Dobbs glowered at Emma in a savage hateful manner, there was an animalistic quality about him that made her shudder.

"I'm done with talking you bitch, now let me tell you what is going to happen when my wife gets back. She will hold your hand down on that very table and I will cut off every one of your fingers until you tell me where its located. Should you still feel uncooperative after that, which I think highly unlikely, I will press your face down on the hot plate. Now, do you get where I am coming from?"

Emma felt violently sick, she was beaten. He would do it, there was no doubt in her mind.... he would do it. Her subconscious briefly thought of the island and the gold she had taken and the wad of notes in her pocket obtained from but the smallest portion of what was out there… then her escape plan came to her in a flash.

"The island Frank, it's all hidden on the island in the bird hide."

Frank narrowed his evil eyes and shook his head.

"Rubbish, you have never set foot on that island since you have been here!"

Emma quickly described the inside of the boathouse and bird hide in copious detail. This satisfied him and he laughed.

"I see you have been busy on your walks. What is over there? Gold or silver?" Emma slowly reached for the wad of notes while talking.

"No, its cash, hidden in two suitcases encased in airtight bags under the floorboards, I could only open one of them."

Frank seemed slightly dubious of it being cash and was on the point of another outburst.

It's true Frank I swear! Look, I pulled this lot out of the case I opened."

Emma produced the notes and adroitly tossed them onto the kitchen worktop next to Dobbs while being careful not to alarm him. Emma had given herself the tiny window of opportunity she needed. Frank Dobbs was distracted by the hefty roll of notes hitting the worktop and averted his eyes while inadvertently lowering the barrels of the shotgun. In a split-second, Emma had grasped the handle of the piping hot teapot swung it round and launched it directly at the head of the still unsuspecting Dobbs. The weighty teapot connected with Dobb's forehead as a horrid thump would confirm. However, it did not break but the lid was dislodged and a good measure of the scalding stewed tea covered Dobbs right cheek and head. He recoiled and howled in pain. Emma sprang to her feet like a panther and knocked the gun from his hand. Dobbs launched a counter-attack with his right fist but Emma blocked this then secured his fingers in her hand and bent them back not letting go.

"You learn little moves like this Frank when you are dating a bloke whose idea of ending an evening drinking with his mates is to go home and plaster his girlfriend's nose over her face! Now, do you see where I am coming from?"

Dobbs tried to grab Emma with his left hand but she increased the backwards push on his fingers and in conjunction with this brought her knee up into his groin as he bent forward in pain. She again brought her knee up into his face sending him backwards onto the hard floor. Before she could claim the gun for herself, the back door was flung open and Pam stumbled onto the scene.

"Sorry I took so long Frank it's so slippery out there"

Pam then stopped immediately as Emma advanced on her.

"You little bitch you can join your uncle now!"

Pam's movements were ungainly and she telegraphed

her attacks so Emma could easily block them. After a few jabs, then an uppercut, Pam was almost beaten but she took a run at Emma perhaps hoping to win by pinning her down using her weight advantage. Emma sidestepped the charging woman and delivered a chop to the back of the neck and a sweeping leg movement brought Pam down to the cold floor striking her head on the unforgiving table leg in the process. Without wasting a second Emma remembered the shotgun, but it was too late Frank had regained consciousness and was about to swing it round in her direction. The open back door made it easy for Emma to dive out of just in time to hear the blast go off and pellets scatter.

Emma immediately ran for the garage; the night was bitter and confusing in the numbing fog. Frank would be making his way over to the vehicles it was rather an obvious move on her part. A quick try of the car doors confirmed all were locked, her mind raced - what now? She edged slowly in front of the building but in doing so set off a motion light and was perfectly illuminated. Emma darted as fast as possible and headed for the rear of the stable block and the safety of darkness before another shot rang out. Suddenly she remembered her phone, although the signal was almost non-existent on the estate, it could still generate an emergency call. Then she realised with a nauseating disappointment that both the phone and her keys were on the bedside table in her room. This crushing realisation also quashed her second idea of obtaining a weapon from the storage shed. The only thing of any use was a tiny LED torch not much bigger than her middle finger that she had habitually carried with her since staying in the shadowy mansion. Suddenly Frank Dobbs malevolent voice cut the stillness of the frigid air.

"I know you haven't got your phone Emma, I checked when I was upstairs. You're cut off completely and if you try and make a run for it, I will gun you down, there isn't a place I don't know on the estate and don't forget the front gates are locked. Are you over by the stables? That would be ironic because that's what I had planned for you, kicked in the head while trying to mount one of Heathcoat's dotty nags… wouldn't have taken much, just sit you behind the colt and shout in its ear."

Emma was shivering uncontrollably - her only option now was to make off over the fields she was a sitting duck at the moment. Working on dead reckoning from the last word spoken by the murderer Dobbs and even allowing for the muffling fog, Emma fixed his position as being in the front courtyard with his back to the house and near the last stall in the stable block.

Emma hugged the dark rear wall of the stables and made her way round to the end storage room. It wasn't easy trying to remain silent – the frozen snow crunched under her weight and that combined with the trail of footprints that she was helplessly leaving, threatened to give her searcher an instant clue. Finally, she reached the roller shutters indicating she was outside the storage shed. She listened intently but heard nothing, the blackness of the parkland beyond the stables looked foreboding but it was her only chance. Emma counted to three in her mind and then sprinted out of her hiding place being careful to avoid

icy patches which would send her effortlessly to the ground
and present Dobbs with an easy kill.

Emma gained the parkland in no time and kept going -
she planned to run another two hundred feet or so then
sharply veer off and head to the gatehouse to use the
Dobb's own phone to call the police. The gatehouse would
be empty now as she was pretty sure Pam was out for the
duration, also she didn't want to give Frank a straight
course to follow. The locked gates were high but she was
reasonably confident about scaling them. Any minute
Emma expected to hear shots, but that was ridiculous
because they say you don't hear the shot that kills you!
Although she knew how detrimental it was to her escape,
she couldn't help to steal a glance back to see if Frank was
in pursuit, shotgun and torch in hand. A snatched look back
showed nothing but before she could turn her head back
and pour on more speed, she collided with something and
careened to the snowy ground winded and dazed.

The "something" that Emma had run full blast into was,
in fact, a "someone." This unknown personage was also
feeling the effects of the collision but had recovered
sufficiently to advance on Emma's stricken body until
almost directly over her. Emma knew it was the end. Frank
had worked out what she was planning and outflanked her,
he must have been waiting for her to literally run into his
arms. She was now far too dangerous to be kept alive a
minute longer, her end would be delivered by means of a
shotgun at point-blank range. Emma had never been
religious but she prayed to God it would be quick and
would shed no tears in the seconds that remained of her

life.

"Get it over with you pathetic coward, I'm getting cold down here!"

"Emma is that you? What in the name of thunder are you doing? And come to think of it what is going on around here?"

Emma remembered how when she first heard Bill's voice it had invoked annoyance within her but now it was a feeling of indescribable relief - bordering on hysteria.

"Bill, thank God. We need to get away from here and back to your place, something terrible has happened."

Emma struggled back to her feet and tried to take deep breaths.

"Fiona phoned me in a real state, she said you were talking on the phone and got cut off, she was worried for your safety. My car wouldn't start so I walked across the fields, who the hell was shooting out here? And why you".

Another shot rang out but from a greater distance, Bill instantly groaned and crumpled to the snow. Emma hadn't realised but a torch beam had been shining on her and Bill. Emma dived to her right and back into darkness.

"Bill, oh my god Bill say something!"

The thin ray from her torch confirmed her worst fears, the snow beneath Bills inert body was turning red as blood leached out of his fatal wounds. Emma was once again on her own. Quickly she turned off her torch and ran towards the dim outline of a petrified oak tree. The double murderer Dobbs was almost at the area where Bill lay - he may even have thought it was her he had hit. Emma ran for her life again - first straight then she cut back across the lit driveway and entered the parkland on the other side of the drive putting the mansion on her left. She had to get back inside and collect her bunch of keys – on it was a spare ignition key to the Range Rover she had been driving.

Staying in darkness until the last possible moment Emma darted towards her own frozen car at the front of the house and took cover. Slowly her heart stopped thumping so hard, her laboured breathing began to steady and then common sense returned. She surmised going back into the house was too dangerous. Pam had cut the phones so that avenue was closed, and also if Dobbs had been upstairs in her room, he would have taken her keys long before this nightmare started. It was probably just as well; she couldn't picture the Range Rover - huge though it was - having much effect at crashing through the imposing metal gates. She needed to stay on the run outside but most of all she needed a weapon. Her mind briefly thought of Bill lying out there - murdered because of her actions! Why hadn't she just walked away at the start? Her thoughts of Bill then triggered something in her mind… something he had told her and this also brought to light the location of a weapon and possibly a way to turn Frank Dobbs into the quarry…

Carefully looking over the roof of her car Emma could make out the small point of light from Dobbs torch. He was still in the parkland on the other side of the driveway. She wouldn't get a better chance than now. Carefully she dislodged the brittle cardboard with its snowy frosting from her car's windscreen, being as careful as possible not to dislodge the snow - as this would be crucial to her plan. A glance to again fix her attackers position showed him to be heading back in her direction, no doubt completely insane after realising he had Bill's death to deal with too. Prudently she folded the cardboard in half and tucking it underarm set off once more into the darkness, as before heading straight, then sharply turning and crossing the drive to the parkland and keeping a diagonal course straight across it until she reached the frozen lake.

After what seemed an age the familiar sight of the boathouse emerged from the deathly cold fog, she hoped Bill wasn't exaggerating about being able to walk the ice to the island... Holding onto the side of the boathouse she began her journey after one final glance round showed no torch beam in sight.

There was less snow covering the ice than she had remembered from her last visit but still enough to make clear footprints. From the boathouse she planned to head in a perfectly straight line, this would lead directly to the landing stage - she would only deviate if the ice was broken. Her first few steps were almost doddering in their hesitancy and hindered by having the snow-covered cardboard tucked under one arm while her other arm was stretched out in front as far as possible directing the thin beam of light onto the treacherous surface. She was reassured however by the firmness underfoot and the lack of any audible cracking from below and skilfully quickened her pace.

"Probably not the best weight distribution but it will have to do," she muttered under her breath.

Before long she had passed the halfway point and prayed her luck would hold, the crispy snow coating jangled her nerves as it mimicked a cracking noise under the influence of her weight. She reassured herself to stay calm and test each area before proceeding, the freezing wind was at her back making her sweat-soaked t-shirt from the arduous running feel distressingly numb.

Finally, the first wooden posts of the landing stage came into view, she had made it! She placed the cardboard down and quickly clambered up the solid gold steps and crossed the snow festooned boards until she reached the island. Turning behind her, she was sure a tiny speck of light was moving in the blackness far off...

"Machete," she whispered and made her way to the bird hide if she remembered correctly, she had placed it down to the left of the door before entering.

"Oh, Christ no! where the hell is it?" Emma frantically searched the area randomly clearing snow with her hands. Suddenly she recoiled in pain and withdrew her hand to reveal a diagonal cut running across her palm. Although she had heard the old expression "don't turn up to a gunfight carrying a knife" holding the machete seemed to rally her and level the odds. Her thoughts raced to the next stage of Frank Dobbs end...

Lowering herself from the priceless landing stage back onto the ice she collected her cardboard which would now become a man trap. She retraced her steps making sure to tread in her own footsteps, and as soon as she had counted 25 feet she stopped and knelt down. Another glance across in the direction of the boathouse revealed someone was indeed approaching, there was no doubt the light was getting closer!

Emma laid the cardboard down and surgically etched round it with the blade of the machete to obtain an outline, once this was complete, she moved the cardboard out of the way and began to clear the snow with her hands until the glassy ice was visible in the fading torchlight. Gripping the machete was inordinately difficult owing to the numbness in her fingers but she had no choice and savagely hacked at the ice in a frenzy. The blade glanced off the first few strikes but with repeated blows it cut deeper and soon water oozed up to create a well. Emma hacked away, sometimes picking up sheets of ice with her already frost-bitten hands and hurling them out of sight into the blackness.

"Right here goes," she said and shone the torch down on the cardboard, before placing it over the hole she re-covered it with snow from her excavations and then placed it down well away from the hole and made two clear footprints on it. She had made sure there was enough loose ice still floating on the water to act as a support for the cardboard, which she now gingerly placed into position covering the hole and making sure her footprints were headed in the correct direction. The fit was perfect but an outline remained which may give the game away. Suddenly a yellow beam caught her eye, assuming it was the crazed Frank and not rescue they were only a dozen or so feet away from the boathouse! If it was Frank and he caught sight of her tampering with the ice it would all be wasted. Emma frantically dusted over the outline of the trap door, but it still worried her - she needed something to miss direct him slightly at this point... She took off her soaking jumper and placed it just ahead of the trap, it was only then she noticed the back of the jumper was soaked in blood, evidently, some of the shot had winged her when Bill was killed. Time was up and she speedily retraced her steps hoping the ice would hold her weight just a few more times.

By the time she reached the sanctuary of the first gaunt bushes on the island, she heard that horrid familiar voice...

"You stupid cow you have backed yourself into a corner now! I didn't want to kill Bill but your actions made me do it. Come back now and I'll make it quick."

He hadn't started across the ice but seemed to be pacing about around the boathouse. The chill of the night was eating into Emma's bones, she had to entice him over to the island. She cleared her throat and shouted as loud as she could.

"I win you murderer! I can wait you out here. You have more to lose than me and if you're thinking I will freeze to death over here you're wrong, I have a good supply of paper to burn in the old stove. Maybe I will start a fire right now using a few thousand pounds of what you've schemed so hard to get your hands on, you and that two-faced cow of a wife."

There were a few seconds silence then two shots rang out in quick succession and a faint splintering sounded behind her. "It's over Emma, I'm coming to finish it forever, you're end will be neither swift or pleasant."

It had worked! Now she prayed he had the brains left to follow in her footsteps which common sense dictated was a safe route over...

It seemed to take an age for the light of his torch to gain the appearance of getting any closer. The beam was glued to the floor, was he following her footprints or had he seen her preparations and was looking for her trap? The seconds ticked away, with her jumper missing Emma was succumbing to the elements rapidly, her hands were numb and bloody while uncontrolled shivering gripped her fatigued body. She had quickly formulated a back-up plan should he not fall foul of the hole; she would launch an attack when he was at his most vulnerable, climbing up onto the landing stage. That in mind she readied to attack. The torch had stopped advancing and had fixed on something and seemed to be examining it, the distance away was about where the trap lay waiting - Emma desperately hoped her distraction was working... Her heart pounded as he carried on his approach and she prepared to put plan b into action...

The next Emma could remember was a strangulated scream a single shot and the light from Dobbs torch vanishing completely, then came a coughing and frantic splashing... then silence. Emma emerged from her hiding place and approached the landing stage, still nothing but an eerie silence. Machete in hand she climbed down and made her way back over the ice one last time. She could see nothing yet; her light would be useless until only a few feet away. The thin white rays of her torch finally found the hole, it was now much bigger with jagged edges and no sign of the cardboard trap door. Just then something came into view and bobbed about in the water. Frank Dobbs had survived and was helplessly trying to pull himself up, each effort resulted in more ice breaking off and no progress being made. Emma approached as close as she dared to the cracking ice.

"You were right Frank it is over. Not very nice being a victim of an arranged accident is it?"

Dobbs couldn't speak but instead held out his right hand towards Emma while the other hopelessly tried to grip the ice. This monster was now asking for rescue from the very person he had been hell-bent on destroying. Again and again his hand reached out to her, Emma knew she had to do something, she remembered the jumper if she threw that over, she could maybe pull him clear. Suddenly he reached out again, but not as she had assumed towards her and deliverance, but towards the shotgun laying close by!

Emma kicked the gun away and spoke, herself now perilously close to the edge,

"You really are a piece of work Frank, but its time I finished it forever."

Emma placed her foot onto the back of Dobbs scalded head and push down hard sending the evil grasping man plummeting down into the depths. His terrified eyes stared back at her and then disappeared into the abyss, the weight of his heavy coat and boots proving too much for his best efforts to regain the surface. Emma stepped back from the disintegrating ice shelf but never took her eyes off the dark opening. Frank Dobbs – if indeed he had ever been the Frank Dobbs she had interacted with since first entering the sinister world of Marston Manor was dead.

The machete was also despatched to the freezing depths then Emma retrieved her blood-stained jumper slipped it on and retraced her steps back to the boathouse. The trudge back over the fields and parkland almost felt like a death march. When the mansion did finally appear on the horizon a small army of police cars and ambulances were haphazardly parked around it… it was time to tell her story.

. . . .

Emma felt the agreeable mellow April sun on her back as she leaned up against the rickety boathouse and blankly stared out towards the island. She had not been back since that night and it all looked so different, almost like in the painting in the study. Darker thoughts then entered her head, thoughts of herself killing Frank. Was she now that different from him? Like him, she lost her temper and ended another human beings' life. A tear rolled down her cheek - not for Frank - who's bloated body was recovered two weeks after he had drowned but because she had no regrets over her actions at all, and never would have. She briefly thought about humans, how they masquerade as intelligent and above the animal kingdom but in reality, that vicious instinct to kill is never far from the surface. She had witnessed that on the freezing ice, the all-consuming feeling to end someone's life, it wasn't Frank to whom she was referring... but herself.

Lost in thought as she was, Emma hadn't realised someone was standing almost directly behind her.

"Do you mind telling me what you're doing?"

Emma spun round immediately in response to the familiar voice.

"Bill! You got my message. I phoned the hospital but they said you had been discharged a couple of weeks ago. Why didn't you say? Not content with playing dead on me you do a disappearing act too!"

Bill walked closer to Emma, his right arm heavily strapped and a wince playing about his face.

"Me - dead? Frank was a half-assed amateur; he only had a mild charge in those cartridges, take a rabbit down but not yours truly."

Emma sniggered.

"So, how are you? I'm sorry I didn't visit but I had to get away after the endless police interviews - I was shattered."

"Well I won't be climbing the north face of the Ager anytime soon and my back looks like a pin cushion but the general opinion is I'll live. How are you, Emma? I hear you copped a few stray pellets too?"

"It was all superficial really, I was only in the hospital a day or two."

Just then one of the estates black Range Rovers came into view as it sure footedly made its way over the field and pulled up close by. Fiona got out and greeted them both.

"Hello you two - Bill it's great to see you up and about again. Emma thank you for giving me the Range Rover it was very kind of you, I think my old land rover needed taking out and shooting - no pun intended Bill!"

Emma picked up a medium-sized hamper that was at her feet but before she could speak Fiona continued.

"Did you hear that old bag Pam is being sentenced next week? Apparently, she only went along with it out of fear and was truly sorry!"

Emma gave a little snort.

"Let it go Fiona, her actions will carry their own punishment. Now if you will both be so kind as to get into my uncles' boat, I'm taking you both to lunch on the island, I have a story to tell you."

With the hamper safely loaded Emma helped Bill into the boat and Fiona followed.

"I thought we might have lunch on the landing stage, is that ok you two?"

Bill and Fiona looked at each other - utterly perplexed.

"It looks rather rickety Emma will we be ok?"

Emma stifled a chuckle,

"Trust me Fiona, it will support the three of us very comfortably."

Emma Maynard never spent another night in the foreboding mansion but instead took up residence in Orchard cottage while she "considered her options" as the solicitor had phrased it. When her few friends asked her how she was getting on and if she felt intimidated with the size and responsibilities of the estate Emma would dryly reply:

"I'm just taking one step at a time"

A dying distant relative with a chequered past leaves a mystery behind and the key to a fortune waiting to be unlocked. As with most acts of kindness, there is always a price to pay, unfortunately, this particular act almost came with the ultimate toll for the person who unlocked the secret. Emma Maynard will now go through the rest of her life with her guard well and truly up and take nothing at face value. At night when sleep alludes her Emma will long ponder the question…when does self-defence become murder?

VOICES FROM OBLIVION

We are all guilty of being complacent at times...but what if you found yourself part of an investigation into ungodly events at a remote building and you quickly discovered that it would be far removed from another repetitious unremarkable inquiry? What would you do if you found out too late that your same complacent attitude had made you foolishly unguarded and something sinister and malevolent marked your ill-considered preparations...?

I'm sure many of you are aware of a certain genre of films loosely described as "found footage". This in its most basic terms consists of the audience being made aware of the characters fate through the showing of their camera footage which is always conveniently recovered a short while later...

A Mr Wadebridge from the West Country was good enough to allow me to listen and take copious notes of a much earlier form of "found footage" he stumbled upon while in pursuit of his hobby of collecting vintage electrical goods of all forms. The arrival of this footage was delivered in the form of audio tapes purchased through a popular online auction room and came complete with four obsolete Dictaphones circa early 1980's. The transcripts you are about to read have ONLY been edited for ease of reading to omit unnecessary and lengthy portions. I will also use initials for extra clarity as to identify who is speaking.

"Audio recording of the investigation of Hall farm by the invitation of the current owner. My name is Brian Stepping, founder and chairman of Third Dimension paranormal society. Also present on the vigil are: Mathew Tate, Jack Dent and Alice Hope. We are now outside Hall Farm time being 17.00 hours Friday October 20th 1984"

BS. "Ok quiet a minute please. Right we are now in the front living- room with the current owner of the property Mr Phillip Oakes. Mr Oakes would you be able to tell us briefly about the history of Hall farm and how you came to own it please"

"Hello... ermm well I bought the property about five months ago through a local estate agent. It had been unoccupied for some time. I own a much larger farm a few miles away and wanted to downsize and retire here.

(unintelligible section and muffled voices at this point)

BS. "Well I'm not sure if we caught that on tape but Mathew heard sounds from upstairs and Mr Oakes assures us no one is up there so it looks like a busy night ahead. Can you tell me about the history of the property please Mr Oakes?"

"Well I don't really know much sorry; it was built in the 1930's but the barn is much older oh, and the land is about 30 acres in total. The last owner rented out the property at various points and people seem to have come and gone randomly."

BS. "So, a classic scenario of no one staying long. Finally, can you tell us what you have experienced since buying and staying in the house?"

"Well I don't actually live here full time; my plan was to fully modernise and decorate the house before moving in. I have spent several nights here and find myself at a loose end to explain what I have experienced.

(brief pause and general chatter at this point before Mr Oakes starts talking again)

"I would say it was the fourth or fifth night I was staying over. I had noticed my Spaniel was very edgy and nervous. I spent most of the day stripping wallpaper in the kitchen when at random times I would hear footsteps upstairs – I went up to look more times than I can remember but no one was there. I also noticed from that day the awful feeling of being watched. My wife won't set foot near the place after waking one night to get a glass of water, she swears blind a black cloud or mass was swirling round the rooms and followed her into the kitchen. I'm at a loss what to do really, things seem to be getting worse. I very much doubt we will retire here now even if things were normal".

(First tape ends at this point and we pick up the next entry after Mr Oakes has left the property)

BS. "For the record Mr Oakes has shown us around the site and now left. He will be back tomorrow morning at 7am. A brief rundown of the property for our notes. Main hall, living room on the left, another room of equal size on the right, both with only a scattering of furniture. End of the hall is the kitchen and walk-in pantry. Upstairs there are two good-sized bedrooms, a smaller box room and finally the bathroom and toilet".

(Brian Stepping then goes on a brief walk of the house and explains that each member of the team will be carrying their own Dictaphone to record their experiences and any unexplained noises throughout the night. It is also obvious he has rather a cavalier attitude at times. Let's pick things up at a little past 9pm in the upstairs' rooms with investigator Jack Dent.)

JD. "Investigation of upstairs rooms with myself and also present is Alice, time now is 9.15 pm. We are both currently in the back bedroom having first checked the other upstairs rooms. Should be noted that there is a very significant temperature drop upstairs but we have dismissed this due to the fact the only heating in the building is from the coal fire downstairs. The boiler is not functional and has not yet been recommissioned by the owner. I'm really not expecting to catch anything other than a cold at this place".

(Very little happens for the next hour other than some brief chatting and another walk round the upstairs rooms.)

JD. "Time 10.17pm and we can hear a tapping noise but as yet cannot discern where its originating from. It seems like its all-around us".

(several muffled thuds can be heard at this point on the tape)

JD. "Alice is going to check the other rooms while I remain recording here".

AH. "I'm now in the front bedroom and can hear scratching from the walls and a tapping noise. It seems to be everywhere at once! The room is not in darkness I can see every corner but nothing is visible.

(unintelligible short section)

AH. I don't like this – whatever it is it seems to be inside the walls or something. Hey wait… the door has just closed, I left it slightly ajar. I'm locked in. I'm trying the door but, oh no! the lights have just gone out".

(unintelligible section with random knocking and

curious scratching noises.)

JD. "Moving to the front bedroom I can hear Alice calling out, noises still ongoing. Alice step away from the door I'm coming in. What on earth is going on? Why are you in darkness?"

(Both tapes seem to have been switched off at this point and resume again at just after 11pm)

AH." For the record I do not feel comfortable in this house. A short while ago I was investigating the front room when I was suddenly locked in and the lights went out. I'm convinced something was in the room with me and meant me harm. It has been agreed with the rest of the group I will leave the investigation and drive home."

(before going any further, I will include a brief transcript of what was happening at roughly the time the upstairs investigation was in progress.)

MT. "Continued investigation of the downstairs rooms, Mathew and Brian in attendance, time now 10pm. We both have the uncanny feeling of being watched, it's quite remarkable. Also there seems to be tapping noises coming from the kitchen walls, I'm holding the recorder above my head to capture them.

(nothing at first then clear wrappings can be heard – six altogether in two lots of three)

MT. This is unbelievable but the pantry door has just opened and closed on its own with us in full view! Brian is taking still photos at the moment. I can hear footsteps in the living room I'm heading there now, I'm sure we closed this door but it's open now and I......"

(*muffled clatter and unintelligible section*)

BS. "For the record Mathew walked into the front room to trace the sound of footsteps and is adamant a black entity of alarming proportion was sat bolt upright in the armchair. He said it was visible only for a second. Time now 10.15pm, also note the feeling of being watched is very debilitating and seems to be increasing in its intensity."

(At this point Brian Stepping stops his investigation to render help upstairs after hearing Alice calling out. However, whether by design or not he leaves his recorder running. I have picked out the most important sections which consists of a group meeting downstairs in the room opposite the living room.)

AH. "Brian I've had enough! You weren't locked in that room - I was! Something was with me. I don't like it here. I wish the knocking would stop for a minute its driving me insane!"

BS. "Look just calm down a minute I admit it's off the charts compared to anything we have experienced before but we have to carry on with the investigation. Jack pour some tea from the flask please.

(*unintelligible section followed by heavy thumps*)

MT. "She's right Brian I think we are in over our heads here; you saw the pantry door open and close right in front of us! When have we ever seen anything like that before?

The most we have had up until now is a few cold spots and the odd creak or two. I tell you right now if you had seen whatever I did, sat in that armchair you would be in agreement to call it off."

BS. "Exactly why we have to stay and document it! If I had known all this was going to happen, I would have hired the video recorder. This place could be more attention grabbing than the Enfield Poltergeist!"

(*More general chatter in increasingly nervous dispositions while the knocking noises continue. Then Alice Hope decides to leave.*)

AH. "I'm driving back to town Brian, just listen to it…its everywhere and getting worse! I will call back in the morning before Mr Oakes arrives."

(*It was eventually agreed that Alice would sign off the investigation and leave the site as stated. Mathew Tate was eventually persuaded to stay on until morning and the remaining three would continue to document all the unexplained phenomena. However, Alice Hope would have her departure rudely cut short when it was discovered her normally reliable Cortina refused to start. Sternly declining to enter the house again she was given a blanket and elected to remain in the car until Mr Oakes and the clear light of day would provide an expedited solution to their predicament. At this point things start to become less organised with regard to time checks and general procedure, also any hint of levity as elicited at the start of the investigation had long since gone. It was quite obvious the investigators were harassed and nervous. So, with this*) *in mind I have condensed and edited the remaining audio recordings into the most likely and logical chain of events I think possible.)*

BS. "Investigation ongoing, due to unforeseen circumstances Alice has left the building and will remain in the car for the rest of the night. I will remain in the kitchen while Mathew and Jack head back upstairs."

MT. "It's really awful, we are standing in the narrow corridor upstairs and its genuinely like something is waiting to attack us up here or pounce. I really don't want to go into the room that Alice got locked into. We are heading for the box room, should be noted the tapping and scratching sounds have been continuing randomly and its very unnerving".

(unintelligible section)

MT. "Feel these walls Jack, it's so cold in here. It shouldn't be this cold – it's not right. For the record the room is empty other than some decorating items. It is like walking into a fridge, I don't think we will stay long. If only that scratching would stop. Both me and Jack are sure we keep catching movement out of the corner of our eyes. We can now hear dragging sounds coming from the back bedroom. This really is getting too much, as much as I hate this room, I'm convinced something is lying in wait outside the door. It's a very troubled building.

JD. "We are heading downstairs now! Something is up here! I've been pushed and there is some sort of growling sounds coming from the walls!!

(sound of hurried footsteps descending the stairs)

BS. "We are now altogether in the kitchen, even with the lights on it seems dark, I can't explain it. The noises continue upstairs unabated. Jack is very shaken after having seemingly been pushed by an invisible entity. I'm sending him out for a break and to look over the barn, as it pre dates the house I doubt very much it will shed any light on things."

(At this point there seems to be a fair-sized gap in real time. I should also point out that having listened to the recordings personally I was surprised and a little perturbed when I noticed the investigators actually had to raise their voices to be heard over the ongoing sounds.)

JD. "Glad to be out of that house I've never *(unintelligible section)* Right let's see now, medium sized flint and thatched roofed barn some 60 or so feet from the rear entrance to the house, judging by the cables running up the nearest walls it has power laid on. There does seem to be a dim light on inside. Not much inside of any interest – seems to have been used as a dumping ground. I don't feel anything minacious. I presume the light source is coming from the loft area – maybe Oakes left a light on, I don't see how to... oh wait there is a ladder in the far corner, I will resume recording when I am in the loft.

(I have listened to the next brief entry many times and I can still never satisfy myself as to whether Jack Dent started the recorder himself or if the recording recommenced by chance owing to the machine being dropped. What little comprehensible section there is

remains only to deepen and disturb events.)

JD. "Brian!! Christ almighty! Somebody help me!!

(unintelligible section and then what sounds like whistling or crooning, someone with sharper ears than myself could possibly even discern the sound of flames spitting and hissing as if licking damp timbers).

JD. "Brian help me! It's not what you think it is! No, no please leave me alone! It's not what we thought! God help me"

(This horror – struck hysterical entry represents the last entry and input by Jack Dent not only into the investigation of Hall Farm but apparently in life as well...

There is another lengthy section missing at this point and it's impossible to precisely determine how long had elapsed since Jack Dent made his last frantic recording to when we re-join the remaining two investigators...However what little audio footage there is left is continuous recording with no pauses, breaks or any signs of having been tampered with.)

MT. "Brian what's happening to the atmosphere in here? It's like it's being charged with electricity! And it's getting colder all the time. I'm telling you now I'm not going upstairs again! At least we can get out quickly on the ground floor.

(muffled sounds and then a clear growl or snarl can be heard at this point).

MT. "God alive Brian what the hell is that? It's going to kill us! Don't just sit there writing bloody notes! We are in danger!"

BS. "Just calm down will you! No one has ever been hurt doing one of these investigations. We could bring a real film crew back here and do a whole series on this place! The possibilities are endless and it's all genuine. I briefly did a bit of snooping on Mr Oakes, he has a huge farm and land like he told us – respected family that goes back generations, there's no way that this is some hustle on his part to draw attention to the house for some unknown reason. This is genuine!"

MT. "Brian something is in this room, it's pure evil. I think it's coming closer to me now… can you hear those hollow footfalls? What's those dim green lights in the far corner? "

BS. "I can see something but it's difficult to….

(interruption at this point by three considerable knocks followed by the disturbing sound of many voices talking as if backwards or out of sync)

MT. "I have to get away! We never should have come here! You don't get it do you? It's been here watching us almost toying with us all this time. All of us are so used to sod all happening at these things we have let ourselves be led into something unspeakable. You can stay here and continue your ground breaking investigation but I'm going – I'm going!"

(Several seconds of silence and muttering at this point)

BS. "Mathew why are you looking at me like that? What is it? What is it? I can't hear you anymore stop muttering. Mathew you're freaking me out stop it!"

MT. "I've changed my mind Brian, I'd like to stay here forever – we should both stay forever, that way it won't get angry. I'm going upstairs now; it's told me what to do. Eternal hopelessness and abhorrence That's its only gift to the world – hopelessness and abhorrence"

BS. "Come back Mathew! Oh god, ermm for the record Mathew has left the room. He seems to have suffered some sort of breakdown. I'm going to find him and the others and leave. I'm making my way upstairs; I will leave the recorder running. Mathew are you up here? Ok, enough now – let's go and find the others and leave. I admit it's too bad here now to continue. I promise we will leave. I can hear something in the furthest bedroom, it sounds almost like a pendulum swinging. The house is now silent, all of the others sounds have stopped but I can't recollect when. The bedroom door has just closed. Mathew stop it and come out please. I don't know what Mathew is doing... if he won't come with me, I'll find Jack and Alice."

(at this point Brian Stepping's breathing becomes heavier and the gentle turn of the bedroom door handle can be faintly discerned)

BS. "Mathew! This can't be happening. I've got to get out of here. Jack where the hell are you? Alice? Something terrible has happened. I'm leaving the house now. I'm at the front door now. Oh, Jesus what's happened, this isn't right this can't be real! The front door isn't right I'm not at the front of the house, I'm somewhere else... It's too dark to see clearly - wait I can hear something. The hall is behind me but the space I'm looking at isn't as it should be. There is something approaching its too far off to see anything yet. Where the hell are the others how is this possible? Whatever it is, it's heading straight for me, wait I can see an outline now. I'm going to see this through... it's here. Oh my God it's here..."

I will now summarise various findings and conclusions in relation to this whole tragic event. I should first make it clear that the police or any other governing body were NOT aware or had listened to these recordings at the time of the tragedy. Furthermore, they were not discovered at Hall Farm in the aftermath of the disaster.

Brian Stepping's and Jack Dent were never seen again despite a lengthy investigation and search. Mathew Tate was found hanged from the ceiling light fittings of the back bedroom. The police were guarded about ruling this a suicide owing to the fact there was no furniture found in the room for him to have climbed up on to reach the ceiling rose and pull out the electrical cable to a suitable length to fashion the crude noose... This would imply the item of furniture used was removed by person or persons unknown after Mathew was dead. He couldn't have been hoisted to his death by invisible hands...could he? The recording transcripts you have just read certainly rule out anyone's involvement in his "apparent" suicide. Alice was a thorn in the side of the police investigation - she was discovered some four miles from Hall Farm in a semi-comatose state. From what I know of her responses to insistent but tactful questioning her replies tallied perfectly with the audio recordings. Alice developed an almost soporose existence after that catastrophic night, to say she made only a partial recovery would be heaping high praise on her condition. She passed away in 2006 without ever divulging any further information.

Phillip Oakes was also questioned at length but his whereabouts on the night were verified by family members and a local shop keeper. The police showed little interest in the reason why the Third-Dimension Paranormal society had attended his property. Their investigation centred around these scenarios: an argument within the group, an attempted burglary or drug induced mental instability (although Mathew Tate was found to have no illegal substance in his system). Phillip Oakes died in 1998 but not before having Hall Farm and the nearby barn raised to the ground and the land planted over with thick swathes of conifer trees...

There really is little more to add. I can offer no explanation as to why the handheld Dictaphones were not found at Hall Farm the following morning. The whereabouts of the devices for over three decades and their mysterious seller is also at present a mystery... no one seems able to have contact details for the absent personage...

Finally, in the interest of compassion for one's fellow kind and being an all-round empathetic man, Mr Wadebridge did submit the audio recordings to the police after the briefest of detective work convinced him of not only their authenticity but also their significance in an unsolved death and the continued disappearance of two people. The police kept the tapes for under three hours and were quoted as saying the following.

"Although we are always ready to investigate any new leads regarding missing persons and their safe return. We are of the opinion these recordings would shed no new light on the sad events they apparently capture, and in light of the less than wholesome content would only serve to further distress the families of those involved. We would be obliged if this material could be considered spurious, any further attempts to bring it to our attention will be deemed inadmissible"

I will leave you to make up your own mind…

THOUGHTS FROM DREW

As this is Volume Two, I thought I would give a little more detail of my wonderful golden Labrador - Monty.

Monty will be three this summer. I used him as inspiration for the character "Wilson" in the story "Solitude" in Volume One. He is a good friend and always manages to cheer me up on the not so good days… Although he sticks pretty close to me and often trips me up…I am of the considered opinion he would follow anyone home for a slice of cheese!

And in the true spirit of things a little bit unusual, and also the benefit of giving someone a second chance, let me introduce you to "Hugo".

Hugo was evicted from his last home as guests thought him too creepy... Hugo is an original oil on board, artist and age unknown... He now hangs in my hall and casts his unblinking eyes over the front door. I find him a pleasant fellow - but not all will agree... As for being creepy I can assure you that although watched carefully he has never been known to move...

OTHER BOOKS IN THE SERIES:

Mysteries and Strange Events Volume One

Mysteries and Strange Events Volume Two

It would be very nice to hear from all my readers, so if you would like to contact me personally, please email at:

andrewjones888@btinternet.com

Or join me on my Face Book Page:

https://www.facebook.com/drewjones138

As with all authors, I would be grateful if you would leave a review on Amazon – it only takes a second, and is so very much appreciated.

Printed in Great Britain
by Amazon

42596969R00098